DEMON

MONSTERVERSE

ALLIE SANTOS

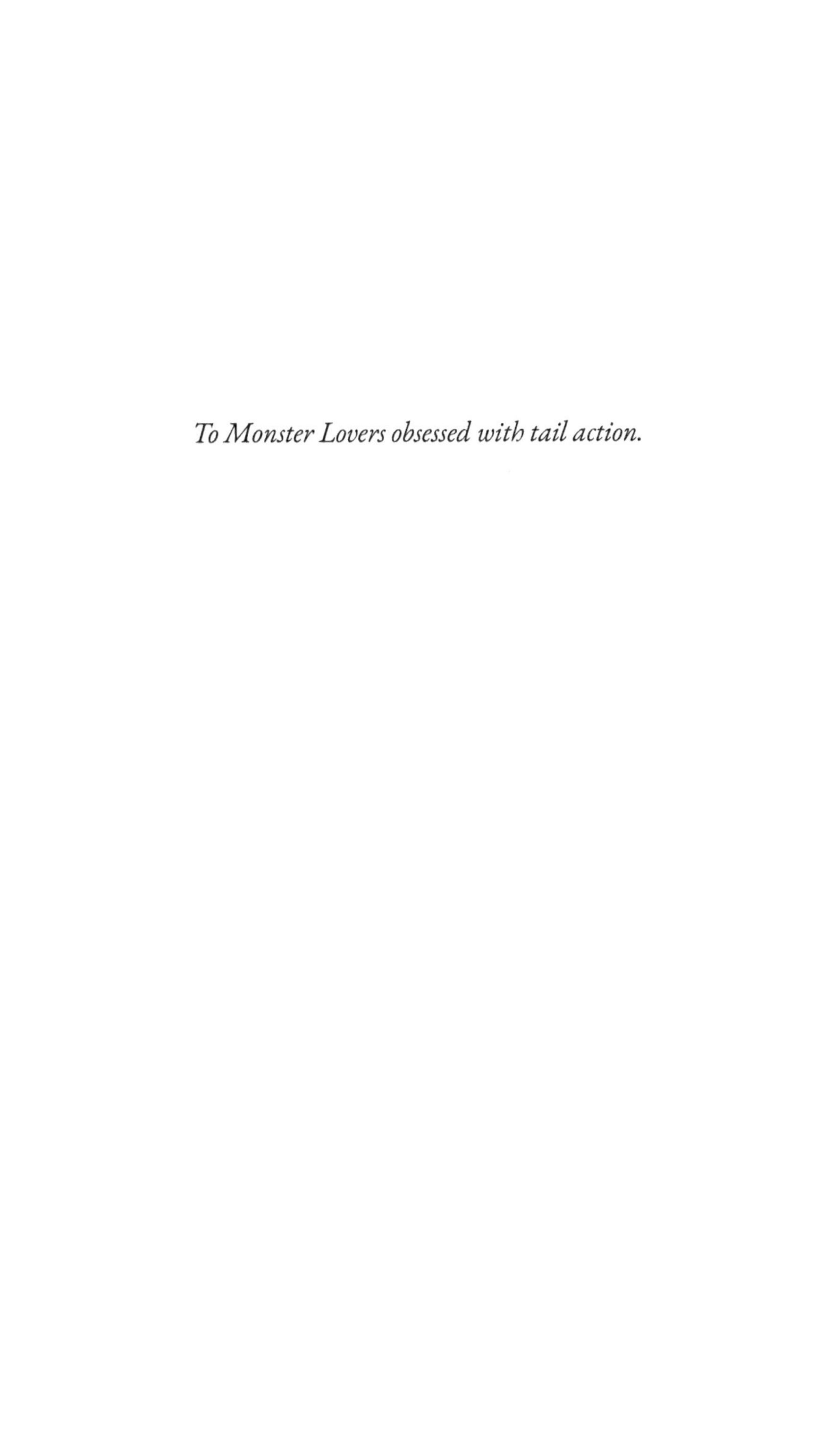

To Monster Lovers obsessed with tail action.

I don't know about you guys, but forked tongues, tails, and horns on monsters make me weak in the knees—and so spawned DEMON.

Honestly, the setting idea came from my fear of earthquakes. I was born and raised in California and I grew up hearing about the San Andreas fault rupturing one day, so what did my twisted mind do to cope? Find a way to romanticized the creatures that emerged from the potential catastrophe.
I hope you enjoy this story of a human falling for a primitive—and highly clueless—demon.

CONTENT WARNINGS

Monster-Human Sex, Violence, Mention of Human Consumption, Descriptive Sex, Foul Language, Descriptive Murder Scenes (on page), CNC

Please be advised that the following trigger and content warnings contain spoilers for the story and plot of the novel.

DEMON is an MF Paranormal Romance. The main characters partake in rough monster sex. The male main character is not human, and there is reference of him consuming a human in the past. The monster performs multiple acts of *tasting* his human without requesting consent beforehand. The main male monster is primitive and claims the main female character without outright consent toward the end of the book while they are around other humans and monsters. There is one scene where the monster is performing oral and she gets her period—he does not stop.

Demon is set in a mythical world and all contents are pure fiction.

PRONUNCIATION:
TENEBROUS [tehn-eh-bruhs]
TENE [tehn]

My wrists stung as I struggled against the rope binding them behind my back. It didn't matter how little I moved, every twitch sent agony through my limbs.

"You shouldn't have done it, Bridget," Liam croaked, the whites of his eyes red. He speared his fingers through his ginger hair and pulled on the strands.

"I didn't mean to," I said through gritted teeth for the millionth time, the pole I leaned against digging into my spine. My voice was hoarse from how many times I'd had to say it, but no one listened to me. "Please, Liam. You know me. I wouldn't have killed her if it wasn't self-defense."

"I don't believe you." He shuddered, closing his eyes. "Leila wouldn't have attacked you."

Bullshit. She was bitter from any affection Liam showed me. His sister was power hungry and had spat her vitriol at me—with her conspiracies about how I held Liam back as she came at me with a knife. She'd said she wanted my death slow and painful, but she never expected me to fight back.

My thigh was cramping, and I wiggled my toes within my

shoes to provide relief from the burn in my soles. As much as I begged Liam, he hadn't loosened the bindings around my ankles. My sides heaved with my breaths, and I tugged at my wrists again.

We'd been sacrificing animals here for years, thinking it kept the monsters satiated and away from our village. There hadn't been an attack since we arrived, so Liam and his father, Kenny, held onto the method with both hands. It wasn't until a year ago that they began tying people up out here when they committed *crimes*.

It was archaic, and I never agreed with it. I just hadn't expected the man I knew before shit went to hell to turn out so messed up in the head. Before the Rift, he used to be a simple, kind neighbor.

I'd known Liam since we were children. We grew up together and had gone through the atrocities of the Rift together, but it meant nothing. I couldn't believe the boy whose eyes used to crinkle when he smiled at me now stared at me as if I were a stranger.

After everything I'd done for the community, they were throwing me away, and it was to the benefit of Liam, the village leader once his father passed. I thought there would be more between us after he fucked me.

Silly me.

Our romantic relationship, if you wanted to call it that, had existed since we were in our twenties—on and off. Then he started changing over the years as the community grew.

My lips trembled, but I pressed them together.

"I'm sorry," he said, as if that would change anything. I fixed my gaze over his shoulder toward the barrier. Dead, dried-up branches littered the cracked dirt and led to dense fog that hid the divider between our world and *theirs*.

Liam turned away, branches cracking under his steps as he backed down the incline. My pulse bounced with frantic pumps.

"Don't go," I begged as my eyes dampened. "Liam. Don't leave me here." He didn't react to my plea as he shoved past foliage. This couldn't be it. Once he disappeared, it meant my death. I didn't want to die, not like this. Tears streamed down my cheeks and dripped off my chin. "Liam," I screamed as he disappeared. A choked cry wrenched free, echoing around me. Birds cawed and wings fluttered, and the trees rustled from their movement.

I bowed my head forward, grimacing from the aching pressure of the rope. At least the long skirt of my dress protected my calves. I couldn't have conjured this scenario from my wildest dreams. Leila never liked me, but I didn't think she wanted to kill me.

The temperature dropped with the setting sun, and a chill lifted the hair on the back of my neck. Shadows, cast by the moonlight shining through the trees, stretched across the ground like fingers wrapping around my neck. The world went eerily quiet, as if it held its breath.

Shit. That was never good.

I shivered, then tugged at the binds keeping me attached to the pole. It was tall and made of metal, and regardless of how much I wiggled around, it wouldn't budge. A small section of cracked asphalt lay beneath my feet, vines crawling out from the fissures, twisting and turning as they spread along the ground. The pole must have been part of whatever used to be here before the Rift had sliced the earth apart. Nature had reclaimed what was once here, but that was the least of my concerns.

How long would it be before a monster found me?

I shuddered and kept shimmying, hoping the rope would give a little. Sweat beaded at my forehead, and all my moving around had chased away the ice slinking into my veins. A throb pulsed throughout my hands from the ropes. I could go for some pain pills right now, but those times no longer existed.

A loud crack echoed in my ears, and I froze, sucking in a breath as I waited.

Was that a shadow moving closer within the inkiness?

My mouth dried up. *Shit.*

Scales rippled and there was a blur of movement too quick for my eyes to track. I snapped my head to the side—nothing. My breathing turned erratic, and I scrambled to get closer to the pole even though metal dug into my spine. This was bullshit. I was being punished for defending myself. My nostrils burned and my eyes dampened, blurring my vision. I could no longer see the inky fog hiding the Rift.

A viselike grip wrapped around my ankle and yanked me so hard the rope dug into my skin and ruptured with a violent snap. A scream ripped from my throat, and my body swung in a pendulum as I was lifted by my leg. I scrambled to grab onto anything to stop my dizzying swing, and my fingers rasped against warm reptilian blades.

A rumble came from the creature holding me up as he shook me once, slowing my momentum. My hair fell into my face, and I sputtered to get strands out of my mouth. I dragged my gaze from the clawed feet, up the thick trunk-like legs and its broad body. Wings spanned behind it, arching and veiny, while the left one had slits ravaging the skin into sections. The monster stared at me from green eyes with thin pupils, and the whites of his eyes held a yellow hue. Holy shit. This thing was like a Komodo dragon on steroids and then some.

It exhaled heavily, puffing out a cloud of smoke.

A dragon.

It rested on its hind legs as it held me up with its oddly jointed hand.

This was how it ended.

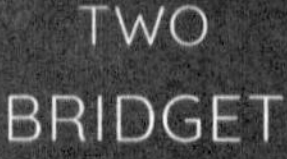

E XCEPT . . . . INSTEAD OF OPENING THAT VIOLENT MAW, it snorted a plume of smoke and hauled my body. My arms dragged over debris, getting scratched up.

Vomit crawled up my throat, and spots dotted my vision. No, I couldn't pass out. I blinked to clear my blurred sight, but there was no visibility through the thick fog as it towed me toward the Rift.

"No," I shouted, thrashing, but the monster didn't react. I dug my fingers into the debris, trying to clutch onto anything with desperation. Once he took me through the barrier, it was over.

My vision faded along the edges, and then I was enveloped by the dark billowing clouds that prickled across my skin until the sensation subsided . . . we were on the other side.

The air felt heavier . . . My lungs struggled to expand, and a hint of metallic tickled my tastebuds.

Blue sparks floated in the sky, small odd-looking orbs.

I'd crossed the Rift and couldn't tear my attention from the ominous inky barrier that stretched like a wall. The darkness spanned both directions and was much higher than I could see. Such a creepy and powerful portal that had rained chaos since it burst open.

"Let me go," I croaked as blood rushed to my head. Did he understand my language? I kicked out and my heel slammed into something. He let out a reptilian click before his grip tightened and he lifted me until my hands no longer touched the ground. My panties were on full display as my skirt fluttered around my face, exposing me. Fuck! I tucked the hem under my arms to keep it out of my face. There wasn't much I could do about being exposed.

I swayed side to side as he held me far from his body, so I was unable to lash out at him, but even if I could, I doubted I'd make a dent in those armored scales.

A glowing dust particle floated near my face, and I swatted it. The speck landed on my palm, and I hissed at the burn.

There was the sound of scraping and then wind whooshing, then a thump.

A large dragon with a slimmer build landed nearby, his talons digging into the ground.

"Are you taking this one to the market?" The words were garbled, rough to the ears, and accompanied by a few reptilian-clicking noises.

Market? They had a market?

"No," the one holding me rumbled.

"Let me go." I trembled, huffing to pull oxygen into my lungs. The creature shook me again, causing my ankle to pop. He moved so quick I didn't realize he swung his meaty paw at me until it connected. Pain burst across my temple, and I gagged as spots danced across my vision.

I slammed my mouth shut with a whimper.

Never mind, then.

A loud screech caused the one holding me to stutter to a halt. The movements made bile creep up my throat, and hanging upside down was not helping.

The smaller one grunted, and his wings beat, sending a plume of dirt through the air. Dust landed in my eyes, temporarily blinding me, and I squeezed them shut, then blinked the sting out. A menacing hiss reached my ears, and the hair on the back of my neck lifted.

The burnt-orange dragon snorted and moved back unsteadily, sending me into a sway. Pressure mounted in my temples, pulsating throughout my head.

"I-I will gift this to you," the one holding me said, jerking me forward and giving me whiplash. I whimpered, still not able to see what he was giving me to through my blurred sight, but the dragon sounded terrified.

I couldn't imagine what frightened *this* creature.

"Tresssspasssssed." Goose bumps erupted over my body at the voice. The interloper's words were deep and ominous.

A minuscule silence blanketed the space, and then I was dropped. A throb radiated across my back, sucking the oxygen from my lungs. I wheezed, trying to get a handle on my scrambled thoughts. I rolled to the side and the stocky dragon dipped low and roared.

He lunged, clashing with the massive streak headed directly for him. It moved like lightning, then slowed, allowing me to see that the glow was a different type of creature . . . The creature slammed into the dragon, forcing him onto his back.

What in the world was that?

I scrambled to my feet and shook out my dress with trembling hands.

The thing had a humanoid body with thick bulging muscles lining his shoulders and tapering to his waist. Flowing white, blue-tinted hair whipped out behind him, and curved long horns jutted up.

He was majestic in a terrifying, glowing sort of way.

I blinked, and my breathing stuttered as I staggered back. What was this creature? Glowing swirls embedded into his gray flesh flared with light as he tore into the dragon's body like a lion ripping apart prey. While the dragon swiped, the other creature avoided the slice with ease. The interloper looked an awful lot like a demon. My knees shook and my chest constricted. This was too much. I knew monsters existed but seeing them live was a slap to the face.

He dipped, and he tore a chunk of flesh from the dragon. The viciousness should have sent me running. Why wasn't I running, damn it!? I was stuck and couldn't get my legs to function.

The demon's wide back rippled with each movement.

Blue blood gushed from the dragon, and slurping caused my stomach to roil. The dragon stilled as its head lolled to the side, and its throat was put on display. Every part of me was locked in place as I gawked.

I staggered back another step as the demon ravenously ate . . . and ate. *Come on, work you damn legs.*

My hands shook as the heel of my shoe wedged on something, and I fell back, slamming onto my ass. He whirled, and before I could blink, he was off the carcass and stalking toward me, his movements lithe. The closer he got, the more I realized how fucking big he was.

The shake in my hands spread to my whole body.

He had to be about nine and a half feet. I darted my gaze around, my stomach dropping to my toes.

He sneered, and sharp, bloody, dangerous teeth flashed. No wonder it was easy for the huge monster to tear into the scales of the dragon. It would be like slicing into a stick of butter to him.

He slowed as he made his way to my side. The shape and bend of his arched, toeless feet optimized his ability to get on all fours.

My heart rate kicked into high gear, making it more difficult to breathe. He was going to kill me. My teeth clicked with how hard I shook, and I blinked tears out of my eyes.

My toes curled inside my old flats as I readied to push off the ground. I had to try to run, but what was the use, he was freakishly fast.

A movement behind him caught my attention. I screamed and pointed over his shoulder at the other dragon dashing toward him. The demon whirled, jerked his hand up, and sliced through its mouth with his claws, impaling it shut. Blood leaked from the wounds, down his arm, and puddled at his feet. The smaller dragon's eyes flicked side to side, agony in its depths.

In a jolt upward, he ripped the lower jaw off. I was used to violence; I grew up seeing it, but this was on another level. A grainy taste of sawdust coated my tongue. Shit, I was on the verge of hyperventilating.

Still, I couldn't rip my gaze away. The dragon's eyes rolled back, and the demon withdrew his blood-drenched claws free from the torn meat and shook his hand, splattering my cheek with remains. I was going to pass out.

But I could not move a muscle—paralyzed by fear.

He returned his attention to me. His cheeks were sharp and angled, along with his jaw being tight and sloped. He had only a slit for a mouth, and his horns arched out of his forehead and stretched up and back. Even with all that, his glowing eyes were the eeriest. A bluish tint that also spiked out in jagged lines around his eyes.

The color was the same as the curves swirling on his flesh. It brightened when they did too.

How was a monster so ripped? Muscles were everywhere, and the indent of abs tapered to a narrow waist where . . .

What was that?

I mean, I got it. Yes, it was his cock, but it didn't look like any cock I'd ever seen.

The bulky, dangerously long appendage had bulges wrapping from the base to the tip. There were about four thick . . . curves, wound together like rope?

It was the last thing I should be intrigued by, but I had the strongest urge to touch it.

His head tipped forward; his eyelids closing until only a sliver of light peeked through a slit. Nothing in his expression hinted at his thoughts.

This was where I should have been running, but instead, I'd perused his cock. I clenched my numb fingers into a fist. My head was on the verge of exploding.

The monster's head tipped to the side as he observed me. A cobalt-blue forked tongue lashed across the blood dripping from his glinting sharp teeth.

"Please don't kill me," I croaked. The demon's head tilted to the other side. "I swear I'll get away from here ASAP. I mean, you just had dinner, right." I waved my hand. "I've got no good meat—"

His face neared mine, and I instinctively smacked his cheek like he was some wild animal.

He froze as a sting prickled my palm. What had I done?

"Sorry!" I flattened my palm to his cheek, rubbing the spot with my thumb. His eyes flared, and something tickled my ankle. A blue tail wrapped around my leg.

I screamed and jerked my hand back, pressing my arms into the front of my chest.

His head tilted further.

"I-I'm sorry," I squeaked, cringing into myself. The only sound was my heart thundering in my ears, and my pulse rose with each second.

He lifted to his imposing stature. Oh, thank God, he didn't slice my throat open—

His tail tightened on my ankle, and he dragged me behind him.

I yelped as I flattened to my back, my arms flailing as I scrambled to get onto my belly. Digging my fingers into the dirt was useless because he pulled me effortlessly.

The long skirt of my dress worked its way over my ass, and dirt covered my thighs. I didn't have time to freak out, because I was trying to get to my feet. It felt like I was having an out-of-body experience, watching myself struggle. Here I was, past the Rift, with a monster dragging me through their world.

It was not fair. Why had it ended up this way? I'd done everything right, followed every damn rule, and all it took was one fucking crazy bitch attacking me to make me lose the safety of the village.

I gritted my teeth, but the fury was too intense to ignore. Using my abdominal muscles, I pulled myself into a crunch position and gripped the tail wrapped around my ankle.

Digging my heels into the ground, I used his momentum to drag me up to my feet.

I stumbled forward, and my forehead smacked into his back. The stiff surface rippled as his wide shoulders twitched, and I sucked in a deep breath. In a quick whirl, he hissed, and blood from his sharp teeth smacked my face.

"No!" I shouted, pressing my palms to his cheeks, same as earlier since it had seemed to work. The creature stilled, and I glared through my slitted eyelids. I yanked my hands away and stumbled, but his tail wrapped around my waist, stopping my fall.

He leaned over me and inhaled. His tongue flicked out and lapped against my cheek. A clicking rumbled in his chest, almost like a purr.

I sucked in a breath.

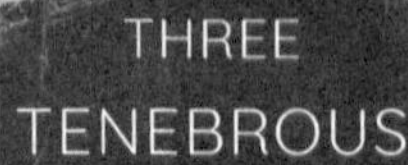

THREE
TENEBROUS

Her scent permeated the air . . . fear. Saliva filled my mouth, but I contained my shiver.

Lucky for the human, I was full and in my right mind. If my instincts were activated, the fleshy female would be meeting a different ending. I had experience with human flesh—thin and easy to rip into.

The only visible difference between my past meal and the feeble human stumbling behind me was the build, but there were no other observations I could make since I had devoured the trespasser too quickly. I'd never encountered a female of this species. It looked too soft and *odd*.

Her teeth weren't sharp and they were surrounded by pillowy flesh. Disgusting—unlike how her insides would taste. The soft pop of bones snapping between my teeth would be the most satisfying. Her fortune lay in the dragons crossing my path, otherwise, she would not have lasted a beat of her heart.

She stared up at me, her eyes round, and I widened my sneer.

I retracted my tail from around her slim form. *What would this human do?*

After a slight hesitation, she followed me.

I had never had a creature offer itself so well. Usually, they ran in the other direction, but it worked in my favor—a convenient little snack for later.

Sweeping my gaze across the expanse of the dirt-filled land, I estimated I would arrive by the time the fog blanketed the ground. The desolation was as it had always been before our land shifted and trembled, upturning the environment. The alteration was slight but distinctive, and the primary change being we were no longer awash in darkness, and light blazed across our sky. If it were only that, then there would be no issue, but with the snap of the portal, sentience had washed across our land.

Self-awareness.

Thought.

Civilization.

Brought on by the merging of *their* environment leaking into ours.

There were many who thrived and experimented in this new society attached to our world, but I never cared to dwell away from the cave I lived in—my territory. Time held no meaning before the Rift, as humans called it, but now it dragged. I wanted it as it used to be: hunting, surviving, devouring.

No desire for thought existed before the Rift, but the day the worlds collided, everything changed. In the decades since we had merged, their languages spilled into our world and it was simple to absorb a version of human speech after devouring the one I'd encountered. The language called English.

The knowledge came without my agreement—I rebuked everything they stood for, having no desire to be domesticated.

"Be careful!"

She shouted and slammed into my side. I frowned at the female. The tip of her nose hardly reached my chest and she thought she could move me?

Her fear smelled sweet as she ogled me and my reproductive member that protruded from my body. I frowned at the lifted sexual organ.

It usually hung in its rested state and did not become aroused unless . . . ah, it thought she was a meal. Her chest rose and fell, forcing my attention to her soft torso. My tentacles twitched.

I stiffened, narrowing my gaze at the appendage until it settled. Madness. They had never moved.

It could not be because of this human squinting at me.

To procreate, the tentacles must unfurl for entrance into the depths of the female's reproductive channel, but that did not happen to me.

It must be some mistake.

I shook off her grip, sneering as I moved away from her.

After a few steps forward, I didn't hear her steps crunching after me.

There was no need for me to turn around to check if she followed—yet I slowed. *Human issues did not concern me.*

I hesitated at the shuddering gasp but then turned around.

The sand pulled her down, reaching her knees.

What had she done?

"Help!" she shouted, wiggling harder, her eyes wide on mine. I'd heard pleas countless times, yet none caused me to pause until now. I shook the disconcerting pull and continued forward. "I tried to warn you about this shit, and this is how you repay me!"

My steps stuttered, but I kept my forward momentum.

She had tried to *warn* me about the sinking sand?

What a strange little thing.

She'd tried to warn *me*, the thing she feared.

The female cursed, yelped, and grunted; her struggles clamorous and irritating. If she died, I would not experience her bones crunching between my teeth . . .

Curiosity was the only reason I turned back toward the struggling fleshy human as her shoulders were sucked into the hole.

A SINKHOLE BUBBLE POPPED, SPLATTERING ME ACROSS the cheek. I winced, scrunching my nose as I sucked in a final breath with my chin tipped as far up as I could. I was sure monster claws would be the end of me, but it turned out to be fucking quicksand.

It had only been seconds after I stumbled to the side that it had pulled me in up to my knees. The thick consistency seemed to be a creature with the way it gulped me. I stopped fighting the strong pull.

From the moment Liam had dragged me from my room, I knew my life was heading toward an end, but I'd been numb and working off pure steam and fear, until now. I'd been six years old when the earthquake happened and had never felt something so violent and vicious in my life, nor had many adults around me. The earthquake had been a record-breaking sixteen point five. It had literally shattered dimensions—earth splitting.

The Rift sliced across the San Andreas fault, opening a portal and creating ruins of many human cities. I'd survived until now. Thirty-five years ago, the foundation of my entire life was altered and I'd lost everyone, leaving me in the neighbor's care, Liam's father.

My sight blurred, and I pressed my lips together so the thick sand wouldn't enter my mouth. I wasn't sure if an afterlife existed, but maybe I would get to see my parents again.

The thick grains chafed my skin and weighed down my arms. The sensation was what I imagined falling into a vat of concrete mix would be like.

I could no longer feel my legs.

Right as my mouth went under, rough fingers wrapped around my nape, tugging upward. Stings radiated from the area and goose bumps lifted on my arms. I remained limp, tears filling my eyes at the scratch of claws and discomfort at my neck. Being pulled up by such a sensitive spot burned, but it had nothing on the pins and needles shooting through my body.

The hold loosened and a gasp for air exploded from my mouth as I landed into a pile on the ground. I curled my legs to my chest and squeezed my calf to rid myself of the compressed sensation. I wasn't down there for longer than a few moments, yet my body tingled as if it had been crushed for hours.

It fucking hurt.

But he pulled me out. The monster saved me again. I licked my lips and fisted my hand in the dirt. Liam, a human, had not heard my pleas, but the demon did?

I shuddered and forced my toes to wiggle.

The demon moved, his strides stiff as each step put him farther and farther from me. My throat constricted. Other than him, my surroundings consisted of barren, dirt-riddled land. Death would take me within the hour.

The demon's bright glow called to me like a beacon. He would be gone if I didn't get up, and then I'd really be lost. Forcing my legs to move, I wobbled to my feet and staggered after him.

"Wait for me," I croaked.

He didn't even twitch, but I wasn't expecting it either. After all, he was an instinctual creature. I picked up my pace, trying not to focus on the fact I'd run after a demon. He could kill me—easily, but he'd saved me, and that meant *something* in my book.

Not sure what, but something. The urge to follow him wouldn't be ignored, and I *literally* had nothing to lose. My thighs burned with how quickly I dashed after him, and I could only slow a smidge as I caught up to him because of his massive stride.

Go back home? No way. They'd probably finish me off. That was no longer my home. They'd turned their backs on me. Being there was tiresome, especially all the male testosterone-filled power trips.

The gray and blue demon held my undivided attention, so I didn't see the bubble-looking protrusion rounding off the surface of the ground until it was too late.

My arms windmilled until my palms pressed into the demon's back, right at the start of his tail, his skin was leathery and rough. The muscles bunched, and I gasped, yanking my freezing hands back to my chest. I squinted up at him . . . but he did nothing. His shoulders lifted and then dropped as if he'd inhaled deeply.

He'd done nothing.

A smile teased the corners of my lips, but I stifled it as I continued trailing after him. Relief was an illusion.

It couldn't have been long since I began following, but my calves and lungs burned. There wasn't a doubt in my mind my body would be a sore mass by tomorrow morning. The purple cast to the sky took on a foggier hue, which I assumed meant the shift to nighttime. A complete assumption on my end, but I had nothing better to do as I trudged after the demon.

Did this side of the Rift even have a night and day? There wasn't a sun or moon or anything I could see to indicate that . . . just a purple-gray tint to the sky and a thick fog over us.

I tsked, shaking my head. Clouds would have looked cool in this sky, too bad there weren't any. A twinge in my side had me clasping it and hobbling after him, my chest tight while his stride remained steady and strong.

"Hey . . ."

No reaction. I huffed, biting back my request. It would be pushing it if I asked a *monster* to carry me, right? The thought was outlandish. Plus, I didn't want to try my luck with him. I counted myself fortunate that he'd saved me once.

I brushed sand from my dress. It had dried and was no longer stuck to me like wet slop.

The ground sloped and my momentum increased. I struggled gathering my footing on the steep incline and smacked into him again, cheek pressing into his lower back.

The demon whirled, hissing. My heart thundered against my chest, and I lifted my hands.

"Sorry," I rasped, attempting to step back, but I kept losing my balance.

My foot slipped out from under me, and I dropped to my ass, shoulders slamming into the ground. My movement took his legs out, and he fell on top of me, wrenching a cry from my gut at his weight.

Oxygen wheezed from my lungs, and his torso forced my legs to spread wide. My dress dragged as we slid.

The demon slammed his claws into the ground, stopping us from descending down the mountain. Thankfully, because the ground would have torn into my skin. I panted, clinging to him as I lifted my hands to his intimidating wide shoulders for a better grip.

His teeth flashed and the glow of his eyes flared brighter like when he slaughtered those dragons. His forked tongue flicked out and lapped against my throat. I froze. Fuck. This was it. I was a goner. My chest pumped, but I tried to calm my fluttering pulse. Son of a bitch, I was going to die.

His body jolted over mine, eyelids narrowing. I squinted against the light, but oddly enough, it didn't hurt as if I were looking directly into the sun—It was more like looking at the moon's enthralling glow.

His jaw tightened, and his sharp teeth flashed at me with his sneer. I panicked and pushed my hand out to provide a barrier between us but instead grazed my palms up his neck. He froze, entire body stilling.

Even with that evil look, the glow of his eyes dimmed, so it wasn't as overwhelming. The joint at my hip twinged, and I wiggled to lessen the ache, but the angle caused me to press my pussy into him. I hadn't been touched in so long, and I understood this was a creepy fucking monster on top of me, but my body reacted even though my brain reeled.

The pressure caused my eyelids to flutter, and I exhaled on a shudder as a wave of need swept over my flesh, pebbling my skin. Oh, shit. I had the oddest urge to grind up against his hard, rough skin . . . but without my panties between us.

I gulped.

Wrong. This was so fucking wrong.

His lipless mouth parted, nose flaring. He sprang off me in a movement so quick he stumbled before he gathered his footing. Without him to hold onto, my body slid to the base of the mountain until my ass thumped against the ground. Fortunately, it hadn't been too much farther and my dress had shielded my skin. The demon inched around me; attention fixed on me as he backed up. I brushed off my skirt, and he took a halting step away, tilting his head to the side. His movements reminded me of a feline staring at something they didn't understand.

To avoid me?

I licked my lips, as he put distance between us. The hesitant movements almost cute . . .

Wait one second. Cute? What in the ever-loving hell was going on with me? I thought a monster was cute?

By human standards . . . he looked scary. Like a creature from nightmares. The horns, the sharp features, the glowing runes, sharpened teeth, and forked tongue were all meant to terrify, according to what I'd been taught.

I'd always been curious about them, but never in a million dimensions would I have thought I'd be attracted to one of them.

But here I was.

I got to my feet as he disappeared into the lip of a cave opening. My heart rate spiked, and I rushed into the copper-toned entrance.

Darkness encapsulated the space, making it easy to follow him as his glowing body strode down a long path before taking a sharp left, his tail flicking around the corner last.

Rocks crunched under my feet, the only sound echoing

throughout the cavern. I needed to hurry before I lost sight of him, because I refused to wander this place.

His glow disappeared again, leaving me in utter darkness.

"Demon guy," I called out, voice warbling. I cleared my throat at the lack of response. "I'm not really fit for the dark . . ."

It shouldn't have surprised me he didn't respond.

I pressed my palm into the surface of the jagged walls, then withdrew them with a hiss. Excruciating cold burned my palm, and I shook out my hand.

"Hello . . . demon guy?"

I tried again but nothing. The knot in my throat pulsated and grew. With my arms wrapped around my chest, I inched through the dark.

Everything would be okay. I just needed to get to him, and all would be well. Shit, maybe I should find a way out of here and run back toward the human side of the Rift. I was way over my head with this. I'd never imagined I would see monsters and experience what lay on the other side of the divide, and staying here would only result in me becoming monster food . . . But where would I go?

A brief flash of blue light had me running toward it. The tip of my toe caught on uneven ground, and I flew face-first into a wall. A cry ripped from my throat as my nose and forehead burned. I whimpered and cupped my face with my dirt-covered hands. Thank God I wasn't running faster, or I would have broken it.

I gingerly felt around the flesh, wincing at the pain.

Forcing myself forward, I went the opposite direction from where I'd slammed into the rock. I lifted my dress to wrap it around my hands so my skin wouldn't connect with the cold wall. Goose bumps rose on my exposed legs.

Was that light? I angled toward it, and a beam of illumination broke through the top of the high, uneven ceiling of a small alcove. The space measured nothing longer than twenty feet long and eight feet wide, and the rugged walls curved toward the slit at the top in a jagged imitation of a dome. In the farthest section of the space lay a bundle of bristly-looking material.

I halted halfway across the space, my fingers itching to touch it. Maybe I shouldn't, but the curiosity won, so I tugged on the thin coarse material and stretched it out. It was cool to the touch, but not the uncomfortable cold like the walls. It warmed the longer I held my palm to it. I enveloped myself in it by pulling it over my shoulders. Wrapped in the blanket, I became aware of the cavern's ungodly freezing temperature.

My stomach growled, and I moistened my lips. It hadn't been too long since I'd eaten but discomfort swirled in my stomach.

I rubbed my face, and a clicking brought my attention downward.

A bug-like thing crawled right by my foot, the size of a tire with *multiple* legs. Like an overgrown circle beetle.

A scream ripped from my throat as I took off at a sprint into the dark. The thing was after me. I took a sharp turn out of that long room.

My panting breaths echoed off the walls as I replayed images of the thing I'd run away from.

A blue glow shone from the corner of my eye, breaking into the darkness, and I careened toward the demon. He spun, staring at me as I zoomed toward him like a missile.

Without a second thought, I tossed myself onto his torso and used my legs to climb up his body until my arms hooked around his neck and my legs fastened around his waist. The material I'd held onto for dear life puddled at his feet.

Oh God, it'd skidded near my ankles! A shiver trembled down my spine as I tightened my cold thighs around leathery flesh. The muscles beneath my legs flexed, and runes flashed bright, causing me to squint at the onslaught.

What was I doing? I shook my head, loosening my grip.

A skittering reached my ears.

Fuck no! I tightened my hold, hoisting myself higher on his cold body even though my dress tangled with my legs.

My breasts heaved against his torso, and his blank features surveyed me. The brightened orbs of his eyes blared into mine, sending me into a blinking frenzy as I avoided the overwhelming brightness.

I shouldn't be holding onto a literal monster, but I couldn't bring myself to let go. Instead, my muscles spasmed, locking me closer.

As weird as it was, he'd become my solace. Although a part of me knew he could end my life, I couldn't help but cling to him.

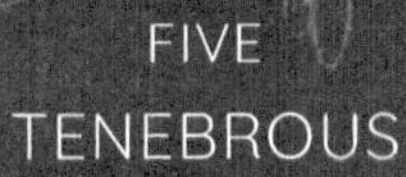

She clung with a tight grip, her small fingers pressed into my shoulders. Heat flamed from each point of contact with her skin. Her human eyes flicked side to side, avoiding me.

A foreign burning scent stung my nose and settled on my tongue. My nostrils flared from the taste as I peered down at the frightened human. She should run from me, yet her body shook against mine.

Her legs flexed around my waist. Was she seeking comfort . . . from me?

Unsettling creature.

Humans ran from what they did not understand. They attacked without remorse, and she should do the same.

Why was she running toward me? Why was she holding onto me?

The human upended every reaction I'd ever encountered. Her peculiar face tipped up toward me.

That burning scent trickled away, replaced by another scent.

Sweeter and mouthwatering. Were there different levels to a human's fear?

It may pay off keeping her alive a few cycles, just to absorb that scent. It coiled through my frame, filling me with a euphoric sensation I'd not encountered. A delectable little morsel she was.

My breeding member lifted and pressed to my stomach until the tip of it nudged into her soft bottom. My visceral reaction stemmed from my intention to devour her.

The human's chest rose and fell in rapid pants, and a shudder worked its way throughout my limbs. Her fear was everything I could have imagined, but with the amount of sweet fear perfuming my senses she should be running.

Why would she do this?

What was her intention?

An ache stabbed through my head as questions crowded my thoughts. This was too new for me, and I didn't like it.

I should have left her to rot in that hole.

A jolt radiated through my sternum.

What was that? Likely due to a volatile reason. Ending her was the only option. I curled my fingers to bring them through her throat and detach her neck, but my claws trembled, refusing to allow me to slice into her.

What happened to me? An expansion in my chest ballooned, and I struggled to make sense of it.

"Off, human," I hissed.

"No."

I stiffened. Never had I been denied something. In my centuries of roaming my world, I had not encountered something like this.

I prepared to say something—anything—but couldn't find

the words. My member throbbed, and I salivated for her flesh, aching to sink my teeth into the skin that released that fearful honeyed scent.

A hum crawled up my throat, and I flexed my claws, slicing them into my thighs to bring me back to my senses.

Just tear your teeth into her esophagus and she would be gone.

I slapped my palms under her legs and hoisted her high, bringing her closer, then dipped my face into her neck and stilled.

A scent only faintly recognizable assaulted my senses. The only comparable thing I could think of was the difficult-to-find Craving Lotus which sparingly grew in my world. Creatures like me who were addicted to the succulent taste revered it.

Mouthwatering. I flicked my tongue out. Her sweetness exploded on my tongue, and I grazed my teeth against her easy-to-tear flesh. The sweetness of the tenacious flower was nowhere near the smell of this. It was like a lotus flower but superior. How could she taste of the addicting delicacy?

Was this why I hesitated? Because her smell reminded me of it?

I flicked a tongue against her damp skin, lapping up the taste.

She tensed, sucking in a deep breath.

Her hips twitched, a damp heat growing where her legs spread on my torso. The potent scent of the delicacy came from there too.

She tasted like a Craving Lotus.

I hissed again and gripped her by the hips, lifting her so that delicious warmth and fear hovered near my nose. She squeaked and her legs flailed, thighs widening and bracing against my shoulders as her palms wrapped around my horns.

My mating appendage jerked, heat undulating as my hips thrust, arching forward. I ached for *something*. I gritted my teeth. The glow of my gaze washed over her face. Her eyes were wide, and red stained below them. I did not have the will to figure out what that meant, so I returned my attention to the view before me.

A thin material blocked the origin of her scent, but my teeth tore the offending fabric away, exposing her—a tuft of fur-covered pink flesh. I narrowed my eyes. *Interesting.*

The weak, terrified human trembled, her fingers shaking as they gripped my horns. I bit back a groan and fixated on her pink flesh as it glistened under my gaze. Leaking juices comparable to the addicting lotus.

My tongue flicked out, rasping up her seeping slit. The taste exploded on my tongue. Sweet and savory all at once. Similar yet *much* more delectable. I never thought it was possible to find something so delicious and unlike anything I had ever encountered. Fear continued seeping from her pores, and with the scent came another gush of moisture from her channel. I'd tear into her soft flesh with my teeth to get deeper into—

No. She was like the flower, which meant biting her would turn the taste sour—ruining the delicacy.

Her thighs flexed as she attempted to close her legs, but I sneered up at her. Her eyes widened as she stilled, gawking at me. The pink flush on her face spread to the bridge across her nose. I returned to flick my forked tongue against the juices, lapping it up.

I groaned. So good. It tasted better than any creature I'd devoured.

My member quivered, so I flicked my tongue out, sliding it

into the warm depths. I had to work into the tight slit, but as soon as I was through, she throbbed around my tongue.

The human cried out as if in pain, but if this hurt her, I could not stop, nor would I. This taste. This human—was mine.

With my tongue, I stretched deep into the comforting tightness of her flesh. Her head fell backward as she thrust toward my mouth. She lay back, but I lifted my palm to keep her from dropping to the ground. I must take my time with her savory fear . . . my knees buckled, but I steeled them.

A sob wrenched from her throat, and I ignored her tormented cries. The human should not have followed me home, she asked for this.

"More. Please, harder, demon."

My nostrils flared. Demon. The word humans had given my species.

Harder? What did she mean by this?

She did not want me to stop . . .

I could only remain still in my shock for a moment before her juices dripped from the corner of my mouth, and I continued taking her essence into me. The delectable taste was mine. Her warm canal squeezed my tongue, and I flicked deeper into her, caressing the flat of my tongue against her walls.

A mewling echoed, and my breeding member throbbed to the point of pain. A human and a monster could not, nor should they, mate. Why was my body reacting in this way?

My tongue brushed against something small, soft, and round deep inside her. She screamed, and I repeated the motion toward the small spongy section within.

Did she like this?

Her thighs trembled at my shoulders, fingers sliding down

my horns in a slow motion that pulsed through my body. My hips helplessly thrust in the air.

I wanted more of that.

This unknown sensation . . . I wanted more and more.

I hummed against her seeping core.

"Yes, just like that. Please."

My limbs tensed, liking the plea from her mouth. I must keep her just to taste this sweetness from her whenever I liked. Her cries came closer together, and she tossed her head back, using my horns to force my tongue deeper. Her liquid sweetness covered my face and dripped down my chin. Suddenly, her legs fastened around my jaw and she slammed my mouth tight against her core. The hugging channel pulsed around my tongue, throbbing as a gush of wetness filled my mouth and dripped from the corners.

For all that was monstrous . . .

I swirled my tongue in the tight channel. Every bit of it was mine. The release of liquid was enhanced, and I wanted more of this flavor from her. My gums ached, and I restrained the urge to bite. I would not lose this taste and ruin it by turning it sour like the Craving Lotus. I withdrew my tongue, and her fingers squeezed as she groaned. Collecting all her liquid was my singular goal, so I continued lapping it until it no longer leaked.

I pulled back, panting as I stared at her now red flesh where my tongue had been. The soft pillowy folds were swollen and damp.

It belonged to me.

Her legs loosened around my shoulders, going limp. Any moment now, she would scream like a fear-riddled human and attempt to escape.

I tipped my head back, extricating the hold she had on my

horns. My tentacles twitched, the pressure and tension mounting in my lower extremities, as if they wanted *something*.

But it did not make sense. I could not breed with a human.

She panted, staring down at me, face flushed red.

"What's your name? Mine's Bridget."

That was not what I expected to come from her breathy tone.

"Tenebrous."

Her eyes widened, and then the pink puffiness around her mouth stretched wide, flashing her blunt teeth at me.

I did not know what tricks she played to wrench the word from me, but it easily came. It must have been the confusion.

This was too strange. I didn't understand. It wasn't until now that I rued not learning about humans. Or even other monsters.

But there was no need for me to understand anything about anyone. I did not wish to.

My member only reacted to the excitement of fighting and feeding. There was only one other aspect, and that was procreating . . .

My body wished to procreate with her?

Impossible, she was not of my species.

How could my body ache to procreate with something who feared me?

SIX

BRIDGET

Getting tongue-fucked by a demon wasn't on my bingo card. It all happened too fast—a whirlwind of pleasure. He dropped me, and I fell to my ass with a heavy exhale as he retreated too fast for me to keep up with him. No, he took his glow with him, leaving me in the dark. I pressed my hands to the ground to push myself up and my fingers settled on the thin material I'd dragged with me. Should I follow him? With his absence, encroached the chill to my bones, and I folded the blanket around myself and thanked everything for the length of my skirt.

Hopefully there were no whatever-the-hell skittered near my feet earlier. I hugged myself.

I never expected to have a demon licking away at my pussy, but I was glad I'd showered before I'd been dragged out of my bed, because he'd gotten *in* there. A shiver coasted over my spine, and I huddled deeper into myself.

The way that forked long tongue slid into my core and swirled deeper than anything had ever reached, shattered my perception of pleasure. I'd thought Liam was a good lover, but I was dead wrong. And those horns? My pussy throbbed.

No! Stop replaying it, Bridget! It only turned me on again.

I rubbed my arms, hoping to get some friction to relieve the cold, but as time passed with me huddled here, it became worse. Sitting was out of the question because there could be weird bugs, and I wouldn't risk it.

How long had it been since he'd left?

I licked my frozen lips as my mind wandered to the demon again. Warmth had radiated from him . . . and the way he caused my body to clench. What would it feel like to have him inside me—no.

It was impossible. How could I be salivating over a monster? It wasn't like we'd fit. An image of his massive dick flashed into my mind.

It hung between his muscled thighs, huge and thick. The four thick, *wide* ridges I could only call tentacles, twitched; they were all about the size of my wrist. Yeah, no way.

Despite my determination *not* to think about how phenomenal it would feel to get dicked down by a monster, my mind wandered as the temperature depleted my energy . . .

I sucked in a deep shuddering breath as I straightened and squinted at the glow spearing my eyes. I lifted my hands to block the blue light from my aching corneas and fluttered my eyelids to gain focus against his bright runes. The beautiful light blue that complemented his gray skin.

I staggered toward the entrance, but the glow retreated. Again, he backed away. I burst forward, ignoring the sting as pinpricks stabbed my calves. My sore legs hated me, but I persisted.

"Where are you going!" I called out, scurrying after the

monster. There was no need for him to have such a long stride. He was so quick, but I followed, my heart pounding in my chest. If he left me behind again, the cold may end me.

My toe caught on a divot, and I stumbled forward, my momentum forced me forward and my shoulder banged into his hard back. I scrambled to straighten myself, and touched his leathery skin.

Muscle rippled like silk over stone, and Tenebrous hissed low, angling his eyes at me.

"Were you watching me?" My eyes narrowed as I marched forward. I wanted to see him. To not have him retreating with every step I took.

His glowing eyes brightened, and he turned away, continuing forward.

"It's okay if you were. I . . . kind of like it," I admitted. He whirled, hissing. Oh, he was *mad* mad. I reared back.

I really shouldn't poke the monster, but I was high off the intense orgasm. I needed to get it together. This wasn't a human I'd shared such an earth-shattering experience with. It was a monster. A creature.

Moisture evaporated from my mouth, and I stumbled back, my heel bumping into the same protrusion I'd tripped on earlier. The room swayed and I squeezed my eyes shut, bracing myself for impact.

Instead of the ground breaking my fall, he yanked my wrist toward him, changing the direction. My cheek smacked into his lower sternum.

I frowned. Runes on his bicep glowed near my nose, and his muscles bunched.

I tipped my chin up, peering at his face. His glow flared, claws digging into the top of my ass. My breathing stuttered and my fingers pressed at the indents of his stomach—abs on steroids.

The monster was Adonis-shaped—times a thousand.

Something sliding along my calf wrenched a scream from my soul. I attempted to hop up, but the silky sensation wrapped around my ankle. I wheezed on a breath, trying to make sense of the tail.

Lips parted, I swung my gaze back up, but my vision blurred. I swayed and latched onto his wide torso.

My stomach whirled and I sucked in a shallow breath. The lack of light did a number on me. I was going to pass out. My knees were oddly weak. Shit. Before I dropped to the ground, arms swept me up.

I sucked in a hard breath.

He wasn't letting me fall.

I gazed into his glowing eyes and set my palms on his chest.

"Thank you, Tenebrous."

The blue glow of his eyes softened, and the swirls in his arms lit up, as if taking from the glow of his eyes.

"What is wrong with you, human?"

I frowned, not knowing how to answer the question. The annoying dizzy spells were only one part of it, but that was bound to happen being in the disorienting dark for a long time. Plus, it wasn't like there wasn't a rock to cause my fall. My stomach growled, and I dropped my palm to my belly, eyes widening.

"I'm hungry."

His head tipped to the side.

"Hunger . . . I understand."

He kept his grip on me and headed through the featureless cave. The only way I could tell anything about my surroundings was because of him. Tenebrous was my beacon in this. He turned and navigated through the tunnel, passing dark holes in the walls that I had no interest in exploring.

Light brightened an ominous circular exit with boulders poking out at the edges, reminding me of teeth. He'd brought me outside of the cave. Tension I hadn't realized I'd been holding lessened, and my shoulders relaxed.

It was the same gloomy lighting it had been since I'd crossed over into the monster world. Fog clouded the ground from view with how thick it was.

Tenebrous walked a few more paces to the right and knelt, dropping me onto a smooth stone. The inclined hill we'd slid down loomed in the distance. His tail swished as he turned away and dropped to all fours as he retreated, disappearing within the fog.

My chest tightened, and my fingers curled.

"Stay," he hissed, and I turned side to side to figure out where his voice came from. I scooted to the edge of the rock he'd perched me on and whistled at the abrupt drop. It was nowhere near deadly, but it put his height into perspective. My heart continued with rapid palpitations, but I remained seated on the boulder, attempting to calm my panicked breaths.

I swallowed hard as I swept my gaze around to try to get him within my sights. Where had he gone?

I stilled. What if he never returned?

How was it possible a creature brought me comfort? For one, he was a monster. Two, I'd seen him viciously murder. Three, I'd *just* met him.

A while passed before a loud squeal invaded my ears. Tenebrous rounded the wall of stone he'd disappeared behind and dragged a squat creature toward me.

My brows lowered. It had stubby little legs, six of them, and a narrow face that reminded me of an anteater.

Tenebrous dipped, then tore one leg off, setting off a wild pain-filled shrieking.

I hopped off the stone so quickly it scraped my leg. My knees buckled, and my ankles stung upon landing, but I pushed through and shot off toward him and the creature spewing gray blood on the ground.

"Stop," I cried and swallowed hard. If I had a weaker stomach, I would have vomited. I fixated on the blood dripping from the torn, stringy meat.

"I am feeding you." He tilted his head to the side. "This is a creature many eat here. It's nutritious."

I blinked at him and opened and closed my mouth like a fish out of water. He was attempting to feed me . . . but still! It squealed and the elongated snout twitched.

"He's suffering! The least you can do is make sure it's dead before you tear a limb off." I clenched my fists at my sides, glaring up at him.

"Why?"

I sputtered.

The surreal experience wrecked my understanding of monsters. He wanted me to explain empathy, but I couldn't drag my attention from his body that tapered at the waist. I wet my lips.

This was not the time to lust or moon over how well that forked tongue—I shook my head.

"It's kind to end his life instead of letting him suffer."

His head tilted, watching me for a few beats. Long enough for it to get uncomfortable. Tenebrous dipped and snapped its neck, cutting off the pitiful crying.

My stomach soured. Well, then.

He lifted the torn appendage and peeled the skin back, flicking it off his claws as he strode toward me.

He lifted a piece of the uncooked meat to my face, and I swallowed past the thickness in my throat. That didn't look appetizing. It wasn't helping that the meat was also a purplish color. Tenebrous stared at me, insistently lifting the meat.

I licked my lips and opened my mouth to politely deny, only for him to slip it on my tongue, claw grazing my lip. Unable to help it, I coughed, and it bounced off his chest. The texture and the thought of seeing it ripped up in front of me . . . I couldn't do it.

His runes flared, but instead of brightening, they flickered with aggression.

"Uh, is there a way to cook it?" He tilted his head again. "Like with fire. A flame?"

His shoulders tightened.

"Maybe I should start with water." I shifted from foot to foot as I swept my gaze around the daunting, *dry* land. I couldn't survive long without water.

This would be a problem.

"Is there water . . ."

Instead of letting me explain, he swept me into his arms and headed back through the cave.

TENEBROUS

REMAINING ON THE LEFT SIDE OF THE TUNNEL SYSTEM eliminated the possibility of falling, but any wanderers would fall to their death—just as I wanted. Various hidden areas lay within my space, and one was a pool of water.

I neared the threshold deep in the cave. After this divot, there was a steep drop to the only liquid available for miles.

When I asked her what was wrong with her, I had not meant the strange rumble coming from her body.

No, I needed to know why she touched me with ease. I was not like her and had come close to devouring her in more ways than she would ever understand. What a strange creature. How could she act as if we were not two different species?

Her soft skin and features were off from what was normal, and those blunt teeth were the strangest of all.

Most disconcerting was how she remained so calm against me, allowing me to tote her about, yet her delectable fear had not left, it multiplied. If she feared me so much, why was she still touching me?

I should not be struggling to understand a human. If she

asked for water, it must be what she survived on and not feedings. A Craving Lotus also had to be preserved in this way to extend the feedings. The human seemed sturdier than the wilting petals of the flower, so she would do well in my care as long as I did not lose control.

I hoisted her higher into my grip. She was my lotus who remained at ease in my presence when all else ran from me. She was different, and I must reward that after she gorged herself on her water.

Both of us would be satiated.

My mouth salivated from craving another taste of her nectar.

The flowing geyser echoed nearby. She could drink from the stream trickling down into the heated pool.

I curved her tiny body closer. A delicacy should be treated with utmost care.

My fingers twitched.

I narrowed my eyes down at her, surprised she hadn't removed her gaze from me. I clicked my teeth together and hissed, but she simply blinked, and that sweet smell of fear seeped into my nose, causing my breeding member to lift.

Only a moment longer until I had another taste. I gritted my teeth. Control—I did not wield it until now. A few steps later, the roaring echo reached its pinnacle as I approached the circular entrance. The ledge fell in a steep drop, and I stepped off, bracing the screaming human to my chest. I landed with an explosion of dirt scattering around me.

The human's chest heaved, and she gripped onto me harder, her legs flailing. I had landed with a thud, but she continued to scream, her voice melding with the falling cascade. I remained mesmerized as I stared at her cinched eyes. A faint charred scent mixed with sweet fear.

I sneered, recoiling from the overwhelming burn. Strange human had various scents to her. She thwapped on the ground with my desperate move to be away from the uncomfortable knot creeping its way into my throat. The scream cut off, and she gawked up at me. I stared down wide-eyed, my glow flickering. Her reactions only confused me. Energy exploded through my limbs, lighting up my runes and illuminating the cavern.

I followed her gaze as she studied the falling water with her pulse bouncing at her throat. Blue glinted from the steady stream.

Her hair whipped over her shoulder as she looked back toward me, her attention fixed on the lines embedded into my flesh. She pushed to her feet and hobbled. After one step, her legs buckled, and I swept her into my arms. Holding the female wasn't abhorrent. Her soft flesh rubbing against mine made me want to do it continuously. She let out a small squeak. Her palm slapped down on my side, but I ignored it. Her lips parted and soft breaths left her mouth. A thundering drum matched the thump at her throat.

The reaction mimicked the one when she'd first seen the water . . . she desired the water, so I would give it to her. Liquid sloshed with my wide steps and splashed onto my thighs as I went deeper.

"Wait, I need to take my clothing off!"

She tugged at the material near her throat, staring at me. This fabric was called . . . clothing? I slipped my claw beside her strange clawless hand, pressing down into the material. Before I could tear it off, she gripped my wrist with her free hand.

"No!"

I stopped, frowning at her.

"It's my only one," she muttered, forcing my claw free from her collar. She wiggled, and I settled my grip near her legs to steady her so she did not slip out of my arms.

Bridget reached down and bunched the bottom of the material and wiggled it over her waist, baring smooth skin. The skin on her thighs pressed into where I held her, and the silkiness caused difficulty to my breathing.

So soft . . .

"Help me down." I lowered her into the water, and she clasped one of my hands while her other bunched the clothing at her waist. I gawked down at her hand. Gray, normal flesh to her pale, strange one.

A mass of fluttering fabric thudded a few feet away onto the dry ground, and when I returned my attention to her, she covered her breasts with her free arm, not releasing my hand.

I couldn't take my gaze off her creamy skin. Another taste . . . My runes brightened and my back tightened. She pulled me out of her thrall as she stepped deeper into the spring until the water licked her knees.

"The water is so clear," she murmured. With a trembling exhale, she moved in the rest of the way, dragging me after her until water covered her breasts, while it remained at my waist.

She exhaled and tried to release me, but I squeezed it, not wanting to let her go. Her mouth parted with a harsh exhale, and I forced myself to let her go. She cupped her hands, splashing water over herself. I couldn't help but watch her exploring movements. She rubbed the water over her shoulders, head tipping back.

A vibration that had never come from my chest escaped.

Her eyes closed as she rubbed her flesh, and a strangely blissful expression crossed her face. A knot tightened in my gut.

What was this reaction?

My appendage lifted and poked through the water. I frowned down at it.

She peered at the water as if looking for something within the depth, and with a nod, she held her breath and dropped, disappearing underneath the surface.

My chest constricted and it became difficult to draw in a breath. The water splashed around my biceps as I reached beneath and gripped her soft skin and yanked her out.

"Do not disssappear from my *sssight*."

My chest heaved, the tension within the confines pressurized.

She belonged to me and could not leave me.

She gasped up at me as she wiped her face free of the water, blinking it out of her eyes.

Her absence from my sight lasted only a moment, and my axis shifted. I did not want to feel that.

Bridget's gaze dropped to my chest and lowered to my engorged appendage. She licked her lips.

Sweetness curled up to my nose, overpowering all other scents.

Her fear . . . my mouth watered.

"Your cock," she rasped, staring at my appendage. Under her gaze, the tentacles flexed. Again.

My teeth clicked together—it was not supposed to do that.

A ticklish warmth originated at my . . . cock . . . It slumbered unless I battled or fed. Excitement caused it, but *this* was different.

Her hand wrapped around the ridges, her fingers minuscule

in comparison. A low glow pulsated through the twitching tentacles.

I stilled, everything leaking out of my body as silence reigned.

My need to devour turned into a foreign one and it homed in on the human in front of me.

EIGHT

BRIDGET

"Ssssstupid human."

The curving runes were all over his body. The mass of blue light dissipated from his eyes, leaving them a demonic black. I stared into the pitch darkness and swallowed hard. I gasped. Frightening.

I *felt* like a stupid human for being incredibly turned on. Although there were no pupils within his eyes, his gaze felt tangible.

Something was off. I licked my lips and bolted to exit the water, using every inch of energy left in my body, but gravity wasn't on my side. My knees buckled as exhaustion slowed my steps and water sluiced down to puddle at my feet. The cool sand beneath my toes made each step increasingly difficult until I couldn't handle it anymore.

This was what being hunted felt like. A gut-wrenching fear spiked through every vein. *Run. Run. Run*—my pulse demanded. My skin crawled just as my legs were taken out from under me, and my back slammed into the ground.

I gulped, looking up at the demon. Tenebrous was

magnificently scary, and he was about to kill me. This was no one's fault but mine. I let down my guard, but it wasn't like I'd be any match for this monster if I actually attempted to defeat it or even run away from it.

"This *ssscent*," he hissed, inhaling deeply and tipping his nose in the air. The lights through his body pulsated and the tentacle where a human's dick would be, moved again, allowing a glow through them.

What the . . .?

I was way too intrigued by that bit of him when I should be running for the hills.

Tenebrous sniffed and crawled low against the ground like some macabre horror flick, and he continued in lithe movements until his shoulders spanned over my knees. When he pressed his hands between my inner thighs, I couldn't look away from his gray skin and black claws. His long hair caressed my thighs as he wrenched my legs open.

Tenebrous's forked tongue flicked out and lashed over his sharp teeth, chin tipped down.

His head dropped in a swift move and his nose pressed into my pussy, inhaling deeply. I shuddered, my fingers digging into the sand beneath me. The warm leathery flesh rubbed against my clit, and my eyelids fluttered as spikes of pleasure rocked my system. A hum rumbled from his chest as he rubbed that pointed nose into my wet folds, wringing more juices from my core.

He reacted as before—as if he couldn't get enough of my pussy.

My legs trembled and fell farther apart with my moan, but it caused him to still. No, he needed to keep going! I whimpered, arching my hips for more. I stilled my wanton movement, blinking at the darkness above me. The top of the cave was so high that not even his blue runes illuminated it.

"More," he growled, rubbing his nose in my wetness and dragging my attention back to him. "Give me more." The lower half of his face was wet with my juices.

His large horns curved back from his forehead while his sharklike teeth glinted. The desire clenching my body had to be some twisted joke. His long, forked tongue flicked across my clit. I cried out. His nose flared and his head tilted slightly, then he did it again.

I bit my lip, cutting off the moan. He destroyed me with those explorative movements. How could he seem to know nothing, yet everything all at once?

Those pitch-black eyes narrowed, and he dipped his head, so his chin and mouth were hidden by my thighs, eyes fixed on me as his tongue delved into my core.

My toes curled into the sand as his warm tongue stretched into my pussy, dragging across my channel. My hips twitched and pressed toward him. He retracted his tongue, taking away the exquisite pleasure.

He had to be playing with me.

My abdomen burned as I leaned to grip his horns. He groaned, shoulders shuddering. I used them as handles to keep him at my pussy, and tipped my hips up, rubbing myself over his face. *Yes. Just like that.*

This was so wrong, but I wanted it. It couldn't be that bad if it felt this good, right? I whimpered when he twisted his tongue deep inside me.

So, so good. Tenebrous's nose pressed into my clit, and I whimpered.

His tongue, longer than I thought possible, plunged into

my depths, reaching my cervix. He flicked against it, sending a swell of tingles over my body.

I cried out, throwing my head side to side as I continued grinding on his face.

My orgasm swept through my core, tugging me underneath a swelling wave. Tenebrous continued licking and shattering my perception of orgasming. I'd never had one this hard.

He hummed, sucking at my pussy and swiping the tongue up the wet flesh in smooth, slow motions. My legs twitched at his ruthless attention, and I yanked at his horns. The monster groaned deeply, heightening my excitement. Did he like that? I rubbed my palm down the roughness, and he shuddered, eyes lifting to me. Light had leaked back into them, chasing away the onyx.

I grinned.

I wanted more reactions from him. I wanted to make his oversized body shake.

"My turn," I breathed and got to my knees and crawled toward him. His glowing eyes flared as he backed off, head tilted as he watched me. I lifted my hand, and his body tensed, eyes narrowing. I pressed my palm into his naked, muscled shoulders.

There was resistance.

"Please," I whispered, and then he dropped into the position I had been in—sprawled on my back. As supine and relaxed as the position seemed, his muscles were bunched, letting me know he could turn the tables with ease.

I licked my lips, staring at the twitching, hard, and ridiculously large monstrous cock in front of me.

His head tilted to the side, and his dark horns shadowed his forehead. The cock wasn't anything like I had seen before and it did not hold resemblance to human anatomy, or even animal anatomy I had seen. It was larger and thicker than if I put both forearms together and measured from my elbows to my fingertips. If that went inside me . . . I would die, no doubt about it.

Bright blue speared between the twitching tentacles as light shined through the ridges curled around each other that formed a thick, girthy cock.

And if it wouldn't fit in my pussy, it wouldn't fit in my mouth, but I could lick it and bring him the same earth-shaking release he'd brought me.

Could monsters even come?

I guess I would find out.

A shiver trembled down my spine to my clit. I should be scared shitless, yet . . .

The little granules of dirt sank as I leaned close. His cock was larger than my hands, but I wrapped my quaking fingers around the thick ridges. The outer skin of the tentacles was cool and rough to the touch.

The thick appendages quivered, allowing more of the glow through. They were moving.

I gawked in fascination and caressed the hard ridge with my thumb and encircled it with both hands. The tip of my middle digits touched, and my thumbs couldn't connect on the other side. He hissed out a breath, digging his claws into the sand. I lifted my gaze to find his eyelids lowered.

The cascade of water continued trickling and filling the cave with noise, but it faded into the background as my breathing increased. I'd experienced nothing like this before, his reaction to my touch was so thrilling it made my pussy throb, verging on another orgasm already. I clenched my thighs as a rush of moisture gathered at the apex.

The tip of his cock consisted of tentacles seamed together tightly. I lowered my head and flicked my tongue against the rigid tip.

Tenebrous hissed, those sharp teeth flashing as the ridges moved and uncurled, unveiling a thick appendage within the middle.

I gasped, blinking down at the bright perturbance within those four uncurled bits hugging it. *That* was his cock, and it *glowed*?

A glow lit up the surface, emphasizing the unrealistic aspect of the rounded mushroom tip much like a human cock, but the similarities ended there. Four knots stacked upon each other made up the rest of his dick. The ridges lined with faint veins beneath the thin, glowing skin. I reached for the tip with trembling hands and wrapped them around him. He gasped, his hips thrusting up and forcing my hand down the next dip. Was

I really enjoying touching it? All of it looked different, alien . . . monstrous.

A tickle around my wrist forced my gaze down to the silky inner side of the tentacle caressing me, while another wrapped around my forearm.

His mouth parted, teeth glinting. The hold on my wrist tightened, pulling me closer. The sharp planes of his face remained stiff, yet his glowing gaze hadn't turned from me. My pulse skyrocketed. He didn't have pupils, but I felt his stare.

Another tentacle slid up, brushing across my nipple and wrenching a groan from my throat. I sank my teeth into my lower lip. If I moved forward, there was no turning back.

Who was I kidding?

My thighs were drenched with my neediness. Since his tentacle had dragged me closer to him, I only needed to dip an inch to flick my tongue over the bulbous tip.

The monster sucked in a deep breath, and I stilled as his eyelids widened and nostrils flared. We remained suspended, and a beat later, I wrenched myself from his gaze before repeating the motion.

Tenebrous roared, his arms buckling, causing him to slam on his back as his hips thrust upward. The bulbous tip closed in on my mouth, forcing itself to my lips. He was majestic with that gray-tinted skin and blue, flaring runes. *I* did that.

A gush of wetness gathered at my pussy, and I repeated the licking and suck. I needed him to come apart for me.

My mouth was too small for it to fit, but I could stretch my lips over the wet, glowing tip while my palms caressed the four thick rounded knobs stacked upon each other.

I dipped my tongue around the small divot at the peak of his cock, and tentacles lifted to my neck, tangling among my hair while others wrapped around my arms. It felt too good for me to be skeeved out by it, and the sight was oddly alluring.

Tenebrous hissed, plunging into my mouth, hands curling and gouging the earth. His hips pistoned and his body shook as jets of cum spurted into my mouth. I lapped the refreshing, sweet taste, drinking down what I could. A hum crawled up my throat. How did he taste so delicious?

He jutted again, grunting. Cum overflowed and spilled from the corner of my mouth and dripped off my chin.

But he tasted so good . . . I didn't want to stop suckling him. I pressed my thighs together, groaning against his glowing cock. The tentacles unraveled their grip on me, weakly twining against the cock they hid. I sat back on my heels and licked the rest of his release from my lips.

Some of it had spurted onto my arm . . . it glowed.

Spunk that glowed.

My mouth watered, even with the taste still on my tongue. Before I knew it, I licked it clean. A shiver coasted through my body and settled in a comforting warmth at my belly—a satisfying fullness. His taste was . . .

Addicting.

A gentle touch slipped over my thigh, and I reveled in the tail twining over my limbs. He hissed and lunged, pinning me on my back. I gasped, gawking up at him.

The change in him was too sudden and vicious. Tension began in my stomach until every muscle seized with fear.

Was he going to kill me?

I waited with bated breath as Tenebrous watched me, chest heaving. Everything moved in slow motion, even my heartbeats. Nothing in his expression changed, but the steady stare caused a lump in my throat to grow. My breathing accelerated.

"Tene . . .?" He wrapped his hands around my neck, pressing hard enough to cut off my oxygen. I scrambled, gripping his wrists, but as much as I shoved, he wouldn't release.

Blue light flickered in his eyes before it extinguished, leaving behind cruel and vacant onyx eyes.

I didn't understand . . . Why was . . .? He was going to kill me. The pressure tightened at my neck, and a sting burned at my throat as his claw sliced into my skin. The tentacle tips grazed across my hip, while one prodded my belly. His ridges and glowing cock proudly jutted at my peripheral.

This may be one of the stupidest things I'd ever done, but there were no options. The demon would murder me cold-bloodedly and without remorse. I didn't *want* to die. I never had. My breathing slowed, and my heartbeat thundered in my ears.

Touching his cock may stop him. Maybe if I rubbed against him . . .

Swinging my ankles high on his waist, I tipped my hips up and dragged myself down. I wasn't even sure if he would reach—

His tentacles wrapped around my thighs and forced me down on the tip of his thick cock. My mouth opened on a silent scream while his roar echoed off the cavern walls. He pushed until my pussy was past two of the ridges. I whimpered. That wasn't my intention. I only wanted him to hesitate. If he put any more in me, it would kill me.

I couldn't help moving. Pain and pleasure mingling with one another. His cock was warm, verging on searing. Tears flowed from my eyes as my channel contracted around him. A comfortable warmth settled in my stomach.

Tenebrous released my throat, and his fist smashed next to my head as he groaned, tipping his head back, causing that lush pale-blue-tinted hair to waterfall around his shoulders.

My pussy fluttered around the ridges, and I ached for more. Tipping up my hips to offer some relief, I pressed my palms into his chest, staring down at the three knots left to enter me.

"Tene," I croaked.

His dick flared bright, and tentacles tightened around my thighs. The additional pressure wrenched a whine from my throat.

Tene bared his teeth and lunged forward, claws gouging into the ground near my head. He jutted his hips, driving his cock into my pussy the rest of the way.

My channel stretched to accommodate him, the heat expanding at the base of my spine and the warmth soothing my insides. Too full. A ridge rubbed against my clit, and I cried out as tears sprang to my eyes.

Glowing bulges rounded from my belly. How was I not dead? Instead of pain, heat flooded my core. I wanted more.

Tene withdrew two of the ridges before slamming back into me. Air exploded from my lungs and my head lolled.

So good.

He did it again and again, rutting over me. He brought his clawed hand under my spine and pressed his palm into me, arching my back.

"Yes, Tene. Yes. Yes. Fuck me. Please." I moaned, and his thrusts roughened. The muscles on his thighs tensed against mine. His tail wrapped around my wrist, cuffing my feeble limb.

Oh, he was definitely about to come for me. My belly throbbed, and each thrust rubbed a ridge against my clit. This was driving me crazy. A monster was fucking me into oblivion, and I liked it. I didn't want to run away. I wanted him to give me everything he had. To feed me his delicious cum.

My head fell back, moans exploding from my lips. An orgasm traveled through my clit, wrenching air from my lungs, and I jerked on Tene's cock, my pussy fluttering.

Tene leaned back, neck straining as he slammed me tight to his cock as it jutted inside my core.

My mouth watered. I wanted to drink more of his release. I could still taste the sweetness. Tene's abs flexed with each breath.

He was in me except for one glistening knot.

I pressed my lips together, staring at the glowing liquid seeping from my sex. Dipping my finger into it, I lifted it to my mouth. I couldn't have stopped myself if I wanted to. I ached for his taste.

My eyes fluttered shut. Just as refreshing as I recalled. I hummed and dipped more fingers in his cum dripping down my thighs.

I lifted my gaze, then pulled my fingers from my mouth on a pop. He watched me.

"I want more," I admitted, hushed.

His body shuddered, and his cock twitched inside me.

Something hard dug into my side. I frowned, wiggling to avoid it, but there was only more discomfort. This damn old bed was getting on my nerves, but I didn't have the energy to deal with getting it switched. At the very least, it served as a great alarm system since it always had me up before the roosters sang.

I wiggled into the hardness. It had definitely worsened . . . Shit! I needed to work through the irrigation system before Liam bothered me about it . . . Wait a minute, I didn't have to do anything because I'd been exiled.

I jackknifed upright, heart racing. The quick movement sent a spike of agony down my spine and legs. That hurt.

Pressing my lips together, I stifled a whimper. My inner thighs twinged. I had never been screwed like that before, and wow. Especially those tentacles. And I really shouldn't be as fascinated about that glowing cum. Monster dick for the win—even though it should have killed me. I wet my bottom lip.

The massive cock should have ripped me in two. How had it not? He'd done something to me, he had to have.

A spike of heat throbbed through me, and I wiggled, but it sent a shot of pain through my legs. I was too old to be sleeping on the ground, at least that was part of it, since the original soreness came from my thighs and well-fucked pussy.

I pressed my heels into the ground, curling my toes. I should stop thinking about how good it felt or I'd jump him again.

He lay on his side a foot away, arms curved toward me as if I'd rolled out of them. Since I spent so much time on my own, never sleeping with anyone, I'd probably inched away from him. A dim glow radiated from his runes, casting a soft lighting, just enough to see the outline of my feet.

The small cascading stream echoed through the cavern. There must be a way the water exited the pool if it wasn't overflowing. As I stood, twinges pinched my joints, and I tiptoed through the sand. I couldn't see beneath the water with Tene's runes so dim, so it was dark and spooky, but I would risk it. My body needed soothing. Plus, I didn't like the way my thighs stuck together.

I would be fine as long as I stuck near the edge, and had seen nothing creepy when Tene's runes illuminated it.

I slipped in and washed my body, working the hot water over my limbs. My sore, screaming muscles thanked me as I massaged them back to life. The ministrations alongside the warmth eased me back to the living. I lowered my hand, skimming my chest and dipping low until my fingertips grazed my clit. How was it possible I was already getting turned on after everything the monster had done? I slipped my pointer finger between the soft petals of my core, swirling gently.

Tipping my head back, I sighed. I was surprised it didn't hurt after everything my pussy had been through.

I felt human, and the soreness remained, but I no longer had the side effects from before—wooziness, lack of strength, and overall cramping that balled in my stomach.

In fact . . . I felt great. I drew my fingers from my core on a whimper. Him inside me—what I needed now was control. I squeezed my eyes shut and speared my fingers through my hair. Sharp pain came from the tugs at my scalp.

When the monster fucked me, his dick had bulged through my stomach to where my skin had a slight glow from his cock. I wasn't hungry or thirsty anymore, and the dizziness I'd attributed to being in the dark was gone.

Was I simply getting used to my environment this quickly?

Tene's tail twitched, and he hissed in his sleep, his large shoulders rolling. The sand was dented with his body as he burrowed deeper and buried his claws within it.

What the hell was this inflating feeling in my chest?

I jerked. Giddiness.

About him?

A monster?

This was too weird. Okay, it was weird enough I enjoyed banging him—way too much—but now he was making me giddy?

I groaned and rubbed my face, trying to get myself back to reality. He'd tried to off me before my frantic grasp at survival.

Water slushed down my body, dripping to the ground as I stepped over the uneven surface to where my mound of clothing awaited. Thank God I'd had the foresight to take it off before everything happened.

Gathering my hair in my hands, I wrung the strands out as best I could and shook the water from my limbs. I was still damp, but it would do.

The skirt of my dress settled over my legs, and I pulled my shoes back on, then turned my attention to the demon.

My body gravitated to him. I shuffled from foot to foot as I stared down at him. It was so weird and didn't make sense, but it took a lot out of me not to lay against his body. I craved him—violently.

My gaze dropped to his hips. It was as it had been when I first saw him, his cock and tentacles hung between his legs, but I wanted to coax him to life.

I'd evidently thrown myself down the deep end.

I crouched beside him and hovered my hand over his chest, my palm burning to touch him. This was impossible, Bridget, whatever these *feelings* were, needed to be extinguished. I licked my lips.

It felt like when my legs fell asleep as I hovered near him, and if I gave in and touched him, that sensation would be soothed. So, I touched him. It was like a magnet.

He groaned, runes flaring at the contact.

"Tene?"

He sprang up, hissing so aggressively I jumped backward. His leg slammed into my thigh near my knee, and a rock within the sand dug into my spine as he hovered over me eyes void of light.

"Ow." I grasped my pulsing knee. A sore, dull throb radiated outward, but it got more dull with each second that passed.

That should have snapped my leg . . . something had changed inside me.

Tene's nostrils flared, a sneer showing his teeth as he hunched over me, hovering near my face.

I licked my lips, and he hissed, gripping my neck.

So, he didn't like when I moved. I stilled. Those sharp teeth flashed, the white glinting with his blue glow. He'd tried killing me before we fucked . . . this wasn't any different. Why did I expect him to change that just because I took his cock inside me?

What should I do?

The answer was nothing. He would kill me and there was absolutely nothing I could do about it. If I were being honest with myself, at least I'd gotten earth-shattering orgasms out of it. Liam . . . had been a lacking lover. I was realizing he'd lacked in many ways.

Inch by slow inch, I lifted my hand toward his chest. Heat warmed my palm, and I rubbed my thumb into his abs. Even as he stared down at me with the intent to kill me, I wanted to keep touching him. His skin, his *taste*, I wanted it again and again.

His eyes filled with light, and then the intense glow subsided, chased away by a tremble. His shoulders jerked, and the grip around my throat loosened. I sucked in a hard breath, wincing. Thank God.

The sneer melted away, and his nostrils flared.

"Human," he rasped, still as stone as he hovered over me. "Do not wake me, ever."

My swallow was audible as I blinked up at him. *Not a morning person—got it.* He dragged the back of his finger over my clavicle, forcing a shiver over my body.

His glowing eyes were fixed at my breasts poking through my dress.

Another round?

Yes, please. I wanted to touch him.

He leaned forward and his tongue flicked out and licked the side of my throat. My toes curled as a low gasp escaped my lips.

An echoing roar bounced off the cavern walls, and he stilled, jerking his head back. He was off me within the next millisecond and striding away. I shook my head, dusting the sexual cobwebs away, and hopped to my feet.

That disconcerting . . . and terrifying roar sounded far away, but I also knew little about anything in perception to sound since everything echoed.

Was something trying to lure him away so they could eat me? Were there more creatures within the maze of this cave?

Either way, I was out of my element, and remaining near *my* monster was best.

The monster you know . . .

"Where are you going?" I called, my heart rate spiking. There was no need for him to move that quickly.

He slammed his claws into the rock wall to hoist himself over the lip of the cave, taking the light with him and leaving me alone.

"Tene!" Damn, that hurt my throat, but that was all I could do. I only had shouting in my arsenal. Teeth gritted, I brushed my fingers through my tresses. A little explanation would help about now.

"Tene," I shouted again and then went silent . . . nothing. All that was left accompanying me was my heart rate drumming in my ears.

I bit my lip, crossing my arms. Well, how unfortunate. The stream of water trickled into the pond, breaking the silence. What if he left me down here, forgot about me, and the water filled the cave? At that point, I could probably swim up to the top—I was thinking too much. I rubbed my arms, trying to tamper down the goose bumps.

Slumping, the rock-hard surface dug into my spine . . . Grooves.

I straightened. He'd crawled up the wall, and there were divots from the rocks embedded within it. I could try to climb up.

I had no concept of space, but Tene disappeared at this exact spot. Tipping my chin back, I stared into darkness as I put my hands out to feel for the surface. Touching the rock, there was no burn from the cold like before. Another change to my body. I felt around until I found an indent to grip onto.

What I had seen wasn't crazy high, and trying to get out of here was better than waiting around.

Taking a deep breath, I hoisted myself up, balancing on the stone while simultaneously seeking the next step to push up on.

It didn't take me long to find the next divot to hoist myself onto. Don't fall. Don't fall. I pulled myself up a few more times. This was much higher than I'd anticipated, and although I couldn't see anything below me—I *felt* the height. My toes prickled.

I gritted my teeth. My fingertips hurt like hell.

My shoe slid out of place and left me scrambling for purchase as I heaved, squeezing my eyes shut. Rocks crumbled, bouncing off my arm.

Shit.

The rock I held onto for dear life disintegrated as if in slow motion. I scrambled to regain my grip, but the tips of my fingers grazed the rough surface. The next second, my arm windmilled as I free fell through the darkness. A scream tore from my throat as I clinched my eyelids together, and the ball in my stomach grew.

Oh, I was done for if I fell incorrectly—My body slammed

into a hard familiar chest, and I grunted on impact . . . My gaze widened on Tenebrous.

His chest heaved as he stared down at me with those impassive-seeming eyes. I really couldn't read anything in them.

His teeth clicked in my face, and then he dipped low and clawed out of this section of the cave with one arm balancing my body. I screamed and flung my arms around his neck, scrambling to get wrapped around him as my stomach fell to the depths of hell. He jostled me as his free arm slammed into the surface and his feet clawed at the rocks to pull us up.

I held onto his him for dear life. *Don't drop me.* My thighs trembled around his waist. After a few more jostling moments, he had us out of the drop and settled into a steady pace as he strode through the cave channels. I relaxed my grip and wiggled into a more comfortable position with my thighs still tight around him, then leaned back.

"I'd appreciate it if you didn't leave without a word," I muttered, scowling up at him.

He sneered, hissing. My lips clamped shut. He didn't seem much in a mood to listen to me, so I stewed in irritation as he strutted through the tunnels.

The light spiked through the darkness ahead, and he still didn't stop at the rounded entrance to his home. Instead, he continued walking for a long time across the dry and gloomy landscape.

"Where are we going?" He said nothing. I huffed and reached to wrap my finger around his long hair and tugged it. "Where—"

"Hunting," he snapped.

I pressed my lips together. He *could* sound irritable. I clicked my tongue and settled into his arms, frowning while studying the area. He went the opposite direction of the inclined mountain. If only I could read his mind, because all this guessing drove me nuts. A tickle at my arm dropped my attention. His tail had wound up and was caressing me with soothing sweeps. I blinked down at the rounded tip of his tail which was adorned with a single ring a few inches from the top. Lifting my gaze, I focused on his deadpan expression.

Okay, then.

Tall trees spanned in the distance, the dead limbs stretching high with flaking branches. Ominous. At closer inspection, the trees did look like the ones from my world if they'd had the life sucked out of them. They were creepy as hell. He stopped behind a large collection of arching branches and dropped me to my feet.

"S*ss*tay here," he ordered, tail flicking behind him.

I jerkily nodded, huddling as his glow disappeared. He dropped to his hands and crawled low to the ground, his feet kicking up dirt. His glow tamped down as he wove through the dead and foggy forest until eventually the trees became thicker and his light was swallowed.

I stared after he was long gone. The crawl was out of a horror film, but the lithe feline movements were oddly sexy.

The prettiest, brightest things tended to be the most lethal. He kind of reminded me of the blue poison dart frog. The striking colors were a lure to others but get close enough and you were asking for death. I puffed my cheeks out and leaned back, resting against a curved branch as I waited.

Hopefully he wouldn't take too long to find whatever he needed because it was creepy standing out here alone. I rubbed my arms, hugging myself. It felt so weird, like someone watched me.

The trees rustled, and I whipped my head up. There didn't seem to be a breeze. It was eerie as hell.

A clicking reached my ears, and the branch I leaned against creaked. In a sudden motion, it unraveled. I fell to my ass, scrambling back. Was something inside of it?

No. It *was* the monster.

I screamed and scuttled back as long rough fingers wrapped around my ankle. I lunged to get away, kicking as hard as I could, but it was no use against the ironclad grip. My knees slammed into the dirt, and I dug my fingers into the ground, attempting to drag myself forward. I just needed a little room to slip away.

Dirt caked beneath my fingernails as the force at my ankle began towing me. My arms flailed as I was hoisted high until I dangled upside down from the branch hand.

My screaming echoed and my skirt fell toward my face. I sputtered, smacking it away from my mouth. I needed Tene to never leave my side if this was what awaited me every time he disappeared.

The tree monster shook me, sending my body into a sway, causing my stomach to heave. I was going to vomit. He did it again, and I sucked in another breath to scream.

A spine-tingling hiss floated to my ears, but my continuous swaying didn't allow me to get a good look at the surroundings.

There was a blue glow!

Tenebrous!

Thank God.

The irony of all that smacked me in the face.

Another shake from my ankle, and my stomach lurched. Blood flooded my head, making it throb.

"Mine," Tenebrous roared, and a cracking resounded before

being drowned out by an alarming screech. I slid onto the ground and rolled, covering my head. Tenebrous had torn the arm off the monster with a vicious twist. My jaw dropped as they battled a few feet away from me.

It screeched, flailing his other arm into Tene, but he quickly swept his lithe body to the side. Dirt plumed as I clawed backward, struggling against the wood fingers still clasped around my ankle. I tried to extricate myself, but they wouldn't budge, and all I did was make them sink into my skin harder.

Tenebrous continued the vicious onslaught toward the tree monster. Now that I was on the ground, the tree monster wasn't as big as I thought. He was leaner and taller than Tene, but otherwise, nothing crazy different from the other monsters I'd encountered.

The tree monster was an apt name. The knobs of his joints were stark, and the barreled torso became leaner toward his . . . waist?

My eyes widened. That was one interesting—

I shook my head and forced my eyes away as I scooted another five feet away. Tenebrous wound his tail around the throat of the creature, and then a snap cracked and yellow gushed from his wounds as the tree creature crumbled to the ground.

Tenebrous latched onto the monster, crunching through the bark.

Well, that took a turn.

I blinked as he fed, and cleared my throat as I turned away from him devouring the creature.

I had counted to one hundred by the time the vicious crunching subsided. After a thump, my monster stared down at me, head tilted and yellow smeared around his mouth.

He crouched, nose flaring as his glow fixed on my ankle. With gentle fingers he broke off the creature's hand and tossed it. I winced at the cool air touching the open wound. I expected that to be all, but he continued gripping it, then yanked my leg up, swiping his tongue across it, collecting the blood.

My lips parted.

I *felt* like I should be grossed out by this, but that was not what was going on.

Clenching my legs together to relieve my throbbing clit, a low pulse coursed up my spine.

His head tilted.

"What is this . . . scent?"

What was he going on about?

His tail wound around my thigh, and he forced it to the side so the tip could slide into my skirt, pushing it up my waist. "You fear me, yes, human?"

Such an odd question. It almost sounded like he *wanted* me to confirm it.

"Ye-es." I pressed my lips together, attempting to keep my whimper contained. He was just too delicious—

Oh, that was lovely.

I moaned, tipping my head back, fluttering my eyes closed as his tail grazed my clit.

A low rumbling hum echoed from his chest.

"I like that," he murmured low. The soft voice I hadn't heard him use before struck another wave of pleasure to my pussy.

He sank the tip of his tail into my channel, dragging it out and dipping it in. With the shallow movements, the sensation was different from his cock and his tongue. My fingers dug into the dirt, and I groaned, letting my head fall to the side.

"G-give me more," I mumbled.

Was he teasing me?

My lashes fluttered and his head remained tilted as he bowed over me, attention fixed on my face. Normally, he lacked any sort of emotion, negative or positive—his features remained blank and lifeless, but this time his mouth curled with a cruel edge and his sharp teeth peeked at me. He looked like a creature from nightmares, yet he wrung the most delicious reactions from my flesh.

I flattened on the ground, lips parted and hips twitching. Tenebrous's claws dug into my thigh, holding me still, thrusting his tail deeper.

Ohmygod, how was I supposed to breathe through this. I was going to pass out if he kept dragging out this pleasure.

The walls of my channel fluttered, and I sucked in a breath, suspended and taut as he withdrew again.

"No one must touch my human," he hissed, and dug his claws into my hip.

A wave crashed into my belly and undulated into my clit. My cry echoed off the trees as I rode the release. I was going to die from a heart attack.

Tene swirled his tail in a circular motion, and I bowed, my vision blurring.

"Tene!"

His hands flexed, but the sting of his claws faded under the pleasure. I panted, finally able to draw in a proper breath. How was an orgasm that powerful?

I stared at Tene through half-closed eyes as he lowered and flicked his tongue over the thin gashes he'd created in my flesh.

What the hell? Even that was hot.

THE GLOW OF HIS RUNES LIT UP THE PATHWAY through the cave, and since I wasn't scared shitless this time, I studied my surroundings, which were much less exciting than expected. The ceiling broke into pure darkness to where Tene's glow couldn't reach the highest point. I flexed my hands hooked behind his neck under the fall of his pale hair.

A yawn encroached, and my eyes watered, blurring the blank cave walls. Amazingly, my body burst with energy, and there was an uncomfortable hollow sensation in my pussy, but my mind had other ideas. Sleep called to me like a siren.

His chest was warm against my cheek as I rubbed against him, inciting a flare from his runes. I peeked up at him, and he stared ahead with no change to his expression. His lack of facial reaction was odd, but I was getting used to it, because what his face didn't tell me, his runes did. The tip of his tail rubbed against my neck and trailed down to my shoulder in a steady caress.

"That monster . . ." *You ate.* I cleared my throat; it didn't seem polite to throw it out there like that. I flexed my spread thighs, to relieve the slight pinch at the hips from holding this position. Crossing my ankles behind his spine would be impossible, so I hung on him while his palm rested on my ass over my dress. ". . . you fought, what was he?"

His tail hesitated on another caress, but he said nothing. Was he ignoring me?

I huffed, scowling up at him, and lifted my head from his chest.

"Put me down," I ordered.

Tenebrous's glow settled on me. So now he looked at me?

I frowned, keeping my glare fixed up at him through narrowed eyes. Attitude toward a monster . . . I could hardly believe it myself. How did he bring it out of me? I must have a death wish.

His nostrils flared, and his attention redirected ahead of him again. His tail applied more pressure as it slid down my body past my waist. It slipped through the small crevice between his abs and me to glide under my skirt. The tip of his tail nestled past my entrance. A humming purr resonated in his chest, and his shoulders lowered. Was he relaxed while I got turned on? I flexed my thighs, causing my pussy to flutter around him.

"I asked you a question." I huffed, my face heating. His tail pushed deeper, and I squealed, shuddering. My hips jerked toward him, and I groaned. His head tipped to the side, and he hummed, flicking his tail again so the ring around his tip grazed my clit. I made the noise again as he withdrew and pulled it from under my skirt.

Moisture on his tail glinted from his runes, and the shine kept me enraptured as it moved higher until he placed it into his mouth, sucking the glistening juices off himself. His rounded tail flicked out as I gawked, turned on to a painful extent. He returned to my dripping core.

"I've heard it referred to as an Arbol," he finally said in his guttural voice, and I gasped as he pushed back inside me.

His steady stride slowed, and he turned into a small rounded entrance, toward the corner of the room I'd collected the thin material I'd covered myself with when I first arrived.

I frowned. That's right, I was so cold when I originally came, but now, not so much.

He lowered me to the ground.

"We're sleeping on the ground?" Usually it didn't bother me, I could handle shit, but the overgrown bug I saw was a problem. Normal-sized ones I could handle, but large ones? There was only so much I could deal with. His response was lying on the pile of the same type of coarse blankets. I took one step back, sweeping my gaze around the room now that I could see what was inside here.

Another step back, and then his tail wrapped around my thigh. I stumbled toward him, losing my balance. My arms flailed, but he caught me and settled me over his chest, with his claws digging into my ass to hold me down. I didn't bother fighting to get up, because I was sure to hurt myself. My cheek settled between his pecs and abs. It *was* rather comfortable.

Each blink came a little slower.

The tip of his tail lifted my skirt as it sought a way under, and it tickled up my leg until slipping deep inside me again.

I sucked in a harsh breath, rubbing against him. The friction of my nipples against him had me moving my hips in frustration. He swirled inside me, and the side pressed against my clit with each movement. Electricity shot to my toes, and I groaned as he pulled out and moved it to his mouth.

I panted, watching him suck his tail free of my moisture. My thighs constricted, and I ground against him, full-on humping his hard body as he cleaned his tail off.

The orgasm washed over me as my channel throbbed. I scrunched my eyes, heaving as I rubbed against him until I collapsed.

Yawning, I slipped my hands to his sides and pressed them to his rough skin. His purr vibrated my cheek. There was a tickle at my thigh, and then he burrowed his tail back inside me, as if it were its home.

I YAWNED AND WIGGLED ON THE ROUGH SURFACE, BUT it was much more uncomfortable than Tene's chest . . . the ground. I shot to my feet and brushed at my skin to get rid of any bugs that could be on me. Hugging my chest, I backed up, unable to see anything. My shoulders hit an uneven wall.

"Tene." My warbling voice echoed off the cavern walls, and I rubbed my arms.

Had he left me here? It had only been a day. Yesterday we spent all day going at it like bunnies, and now he was gone.

A vise wrapped around my heart.

I needed him.

I panted, my chest heaving. "Tene!"

I held my breath but nothing.

Fuck this. I scrubbed my palm across my face and tried not to freak out. He'd come back. So far, he'd protected me and even tried to feed me. That had to mean something.

I pressed my palm to my stomach and frowned. The day before I hadn't eaten, nor yesterday . . . today was going on three days. I had confirmation, something was different about me. I hadn't eaten and was still alive without even a hunger pain in sight.

A soft-blue glow reflected off the jagged wall outside the rounded entrance. Tene. As the light approached, I made out my dress beside my shoes, and I stepped into them while pulling on my dress as I rushed around the lip of the entrance. Tene stopped a few feet away. His features remained stiff and unreactive except for the flaring of his nostrils.

I closed the few feet between us and grabbed his hand. His head turned to the side, and the glow of his eyes fell across our linked hands. My skin against his leathery armor calmed my rampant heart. Questions bubbled behind my lips, but I held them in because I didn't want to do something that would set him off again. The way his eyes had turned black returned to my memory. Death had never felt so close.

His gaze fell across my face, and I dropped mine. My hand wrapped around two of his fingers and seemed unrealistically small in comparison. I took care not to touch the black talons extending from his nail beds.

Tene's other palm settled on my head, cupping more than half of it, and he tipped my head back to stare into my face. Even without pupils, his stare felt direct. His head tipped to the side.

"You have not fed, human."

"I wanted to ask you about that—"

He cupped my head, pulling me to him until my nose hit his side and he forced me to follow him. I scrambled to keep up by holding onto his two fingers and even tugged at them to get him to slow, but there was no reaction.

"Wait." I gasped as my toe caught on a divot and I stumbled. Tene gripped a chunk of hair to right me. I screamed and wrapped my hand around his wrist to lessen the pinpricks across my scalp.

He released me, and his hands hovered over my head, but he didn't touch.

"That hurt." I scowled at him and rubbed my head. His runes flared and dimmed.

"I did not know."

I figured. I huffed, and the pain receded. His hands slowly lowered, and he stepped back.

"It's okay, all humans have a pretty low pain tolerance, and my head has always been sensitive."

"I will take care to not touch your fur."

My nose scrunched. Fur? My lips twitched, and I hummed an agreement, not wanting to correct him on the wording. "Is the fur here also sensitive?" He grazed the back of his claw against my mound, and I sucked in a shocked breath. All I could do was blink at him for a few seconds with my lips twitching.

I swallowed my laugh.

"It can be."

The corners of his lips tipped down.

I was done for if this caused all sorts of butterflies in my stomach.

"Feeding comes first, and then we will speak," Tene said, and hesitated before holding his two fingers out. I bit the inside of my cheek to stifle my smile and wrapped my hand around the two fingers.

He strode down the hall with slow, measured steps and looked back at me every few steps. Those flutters in my stomach spread toward my chest.

I craned my head to investigate an entrance as his glow reflected off something gold inside.

"What's in there?" I continued following him past the alcove. His head tilted in the direction I looked, and his head stretched to the side.

"A dragon owned this cave. He enjoyed hoarding."

"Where is he now?" I could guess, considering he'd devoured those other dragons. I cleared my throat. "Never mind."

Silence fell between us except for my uneven stride. For such a big monster, his steps were quiet as a feline. The soft cascade of water falling broke through the quiet, and he came to a stop. Was that a wall? I stumbled and pressed into his side. It was a fall down a dark hole, and his glow didn't reach far.

Tene scooped me in his arms and stepped off the ledge. I squeezed my eyes shut until a thump jostled through his frame.

The sound of trickling water sounded. Sand crunched under his steps as he approached it, and at the lip of the pond he set me down and pulled at my dress.

I hurried to pull it off so he didn't tear it, and tossed it to the side. My arms crossed over my bared chest, and I stepped toward the water with each one he took toward me. Water lapped at my ankles, then my thighs until I was submerged up to my chest.

"Feed," he ordered. What? I furrowed my eyebrows and shook my head, not understanding. Feed on what? What was he talking about? I wasn't hungry.

A soft clicking came from his chest, almost like a frustrated sound. With one of his big palms, he scooped water and splashed it on my face. Like I had the other day when he'd brought me here.

He thought this was feeding me.

"You think this is feeding me?"

He tilted his head and stared at me. I filled my cheeks with air and lowered into the water. Explaining it to him could wait until later when he didn't seem so adamant for me to *feed*.

He stood stiff in the water as he watched me dunk myself. The tip of his tentacle-wrapped cock bobbed at the surface.

My mouth watered and a hollow feeling in my stomach spread. Similar to being hungry, but not the same because this feeling caused my mouth to water at the thought of his cum.

"Is your cum magic?"

He tilted his head again, not understanding me, if the frown on his mouth was anything to go by.

"What is magic?"

He would know if there was magic since this was his world, but maybe it had another name. My gaze dropped to his cock again.

I kicked my feet to give me some speed as I waded up to him and swam in a circle around him. His back muscles rippled, and he didn't turn to watch me, but his tail grazed my belly.

I floated in front of him and got my feet under me to stand. His runes moved in a flickering pattern as I encroached on his space with his cock pressed between us.

His mouth parted, and I wanted to see his reactions again. The way he trembled and how he roared. I shivered.

Pushing him back with my palm, he backed up until water trickled down his body. My nipples pebbled from the cool brush of air. Tene's attention dropped to them, and his head tilted again.

"You can touch," I whispered, and the tentacles on his cock moved. He stood frozen in place. I gripped his hand and pressed it over my breast. The roughness of his skin surged to my clit, and I sucked in a breath. The tip of his claws brushed against my skin, but it only heightened my lust.

Tene repeated the glide of his palm against my nipple, and I sank my teeth into my lip.

"They are sensitive," he commented, and rubbed his claw against it.

My knees weakened and I slumped forward. He caught me, the pricks of his claws pressing into my spine as he lowered me to the sand.

His knee settled by my waist, and his hand settled near my shoulder.

"I'll show you another sensitive spot." I grabbed his hand from my breast and tugged it down. He allowed it, and his rough flesh lifted goose bumps on my skin. I spread my thighs so I was bared to him. My pulse bounced against my throat and stuttered when I pressed the back of his claw against my clit.

I cried out and wiggled my hips.

His nostrils flared, and he maneuvered until his face hovered over my pussy.

"Is it this bud here?" The dull backside of his claw pressed into my clit again, and I pushed my hips harder against him.

His runes flared and a rumble vibrated from his chest. "You leaked."

"I like it. It feels good."

"What is it named?" He hummed and did it again, rubbing his claw with more force. My head fell back, and I closed my eyes.

"It's my clit," I croaked. Tene dipped his claw into my channel.

"Clit," he rasped.

"T-that's my pussy." I panted as he swirled the claw inside me. "That's where you fuck me," I said, and pushed to my elbows to get a better view. His searching touches stopped. I craned to look at his glowing cock with his tentacles unraveled. "Fuck me with that."

His teeth flashed.

"I must explore more, but I will . . . *fuck you*." Another wave of need washed over my core, and my channel flexed around his claw. He stilled as the suction of my pussy became unbearable, and my head fell back as an orgasm wrenched a cry from my throat. My fingers curled into the sand as my core attempted to suck him in. I ached to be filled.

"So wet." His approving tone penetrated through my fuzzy brain.

I licked my lips, and he curled his knuckle and rubbed it against my clit in a circular motion. His leathery skin was wet from my release.

"What about here?"

My eyes widened as he pressed against the bud of my asshole.

"I can fuck you here."

That wasn't a question.

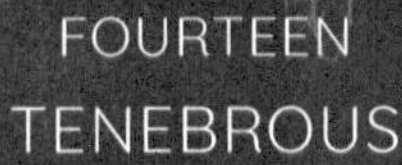

THE BIT OF FUR RIMMING HER EYES FLUTTERED AS HER chest expanded. She liked me pressing against this part too. The puckered skin beneath her pussy.

I kept my touch there and flicked my tongue out to lick the juices dripping from her soft petals. Curling my tongue, I collected every bit I could, but the liquid continued releasing. I was right to preserve this gift. She was better than any Craving Lotus I could have ever found. She was mine.

I pulled back and stared at the heated flesh and the button she called a clit, then pressed my tongue against it. She screamed, and another wave of her scent filled my senses.

The delicious sweetness I believed was her fear was connected to her pussy. Did this mean she wanted this every time I smelled that?

No, impossible. She craved me licking her—fucking her—but she did not fear me? Everything feared and ran from me.

Her hips rose and forced my knuckle into the puckered flesh. She gasped. I could penetrate this as well. The peaks of her breasts jutted, and I crawled until I reached them with my forked tongue.

My lotus's lips parted, and her hands lifted to my head, gripping my horns. I dragged my bulbous tail to her pussy and dipped it inside to coat it with her liquid. In my tail's second home. Her shaking only intensified as I licked her breast.

My breeding member rubbed against her soft skin as I rutted against her stomach, and my tentacles caressed her skin. I should spear into her pussy, but I did not want to stop.

She thrashed against me, and I continued my ministrations. She screamed again, but I did not stop.

My breeding member trembled, and my thrusts became quick, uneven jerks. My tentacles curled around her, holding her as tight as they could with my member flat against her belly. Flames burst up my spine, and I roared as my release wrenched free. My cum spread on her breasts and splattered her face, but I did not stop grinding my cock until every last drop was free and my human was covered in my juices.

The human lifted her hand to my release covering her breasts and collected some on her fingers, then sucked them into her mouth, cleaning the luminescence off.

I shuddered, and my tentacles moved across her skin.

She panted, and the corner of her mouth lifted, and warmth spread in my stomach where I had only ever felt hunger.

Mine.

She was mine and always would be.

The heat in my stomach spread, and I curved over her, licking her cheek as she blinked at me.

Slipping my tail free of her pussy, I slithered it into the puckered section below it. Her eyes widened, but I couldn't allow a second more separated from where I belonged.

I positioned my cock at her entrance and slammed inside of her.

"I will fuck you forever."

I pressed my nose into her neck and inhaled. She shivered, her body becoming supple.

These noises she made . . . I hissed and another release blazed through my cock. I filled her to the brim with my release while she thrashed and moaned.

I stared, awed.

The human was a gift. My tentacles tried to grip onto her longer, but I pulled my cock out and left my tail in place.

My glowing cum mixed with her cream, and I slipped my tongue inside her, focusing on swirling it around the clit. She whimpered, and I wanted that sound from her again—craved it. Her hips twitched and hiked to grind against my insistent tongue. Release exploded from her folds and sprayed onto my face. I licked until every bit of her was clean.

I REMAINED NEAR THE ENTRANCE OF THE CAVE WHERE there was still light filtering inside. Enough for me to work on my little project, with Tene as my helper. I swung the rock down again, and after a satisfying click, it settled into place. Finally. It'd taken me a long time to get this formed, and I had to use some sharp ass bone knife of Tene's. There was one more wood piece I needed to attach, but I needed help holding it.

A bed frame was a must because I wasn't rocking with sleeping on the ground anymore, and I needed a sprinkle of elevation. So far, I'd managed to sleep because Tene fucked me into exhaustion, otherwise, I thought about every possible creepy crawly that could be skittering around. Tene was at a complete loss as to my reasoning, staring at me blank-faced as I told him what I was worried about. Sure, they could climb onto the bed, but at least a platform offered me peace of mind.

His way to fix it was by nestling me on his chest and shoving his tail inside me every night. I couldn't deny it was comforting having him inside me. His confusion was adorable, but it didn't assuage my anxiety.

"Hold it tight," I repeated, showing him how. Passing the wood to him, he squeezed, and the wood splintered to pieces. I sighed, tipping my head back. Another piece broken.

"It happened again." The intonation of his words lilted with disappointment. He seemed pretty put out about everything he'd managed to break. I sucked my smile in and smoothed my expression.

"It's okay, Tene, but I'm going to need some more wood." Splintered wood victims lay around the work area and there were no pieces big enough to hold this slat together.

"I will get some more. Do not leave this spot." Tene stood and disappeared from the cave entrance.

The rock in my hand clattered to the ground, and I brushed my hands free of the dust. Tene had gotten me the wood from those dusty trees and broken them into pieces out front. It was quite a sight watching him rip it like it was paper, and it drove in how gentle he was with me.

I stepped back, observing my work.

The slim board frame was a little slanted, but it worked, I needed to find a way to sand a slat of wood to place it on top.

I dipped to grab the little knife I'd set to the side. Within the pile of wood, there had to be one good enough to sand down. I'd get to the *how* of it later.

I licked my dry lips as I stepped into the dull atmosphere. The only thing I seemed to crave was my demon. I hated being separated from him. A throb of lust had me stopping to collect myself. It didn't hurt that the demon knew how to fuck and make me come over and over again. It made each encounter with Liam laughable.

The tan dirt crunched beneath my footsteps, and I shook out the dust from my dress. It was coming up on time to wash it. I rounded the rock blocking the entrance to where the various pieces of wood lay. I had to give it to Tene, as soon as I told him I needed something, he went above and beyond to get it.

One of the top pieces was large enough for the surface. It was wide enough to hold Tene and me—

"Huuuuman."

I whirled and screamed, backing up so quickly I fell over. My ass cushioned my fall, and I winced, using my heels to push myself backward as the two-legged creature skulked closer.

Her breasts were ridiculously endowed, those curves . . . The demoness hissed down at me.

He had seemed sexually clueless, so it'd led me to assume he had no experience, but that probably meant he had no experience with a human. A demoness probably worked differently . . . even though I highly doubted it since she screamed femininity.

"Tene," I called out, voice rasping. I took in the woman. She was smaller than Tene but a good head bigger than me. I'd even say she was petite for her species.

"Tene?" She sneered, slinking closer. "What are you doing in my home?"

Was this . . . was this Tene's demoness?

He had a demoness?!

I was going to vomit. Here I was building a bed for us, but, but he had her! This oddly alluring female demon.

She loomed over me, and her tongue flicked out against my cheek.

"I craved a snack."

She went flying in a whirlwind, and I gawked up at a brightly glowing Tene. The enhanced shine almost blinded me, but I forced myself to scramble behind him and grip onto his arm.

The demoness brushed off her sleek hair and strutted close again. A layer of skin, similar in texture to Tene's, covered her head to toe and she was naked.

I cleared my throat, avoiding her large breasts as my fingers flexed on Tene's arm.

"Who is she, Tene?" My voice squeaked, but how could it not, her talons looked like they could slice through my throat without a second thought.

"You were not to return for a long while," Tene said, head tilting to the side.

I huffed. What did that mean? His mass of hair fluttered over his shoulder. I scowled, and my fingers went limp, sliding off his arm. An uncomfortable balloon inflated in my stomach, expanding and pushing to my throat.

"I returned." She huffed and crossed her arms.

Who the hell was she?

I was about to start swinging, which was a bad move since, *hello*, they were demons. I gritted my teeth and tapped my foot.

Tene finally, *finally* looked over his shoulder at me.

"Get inside."

He gripped my arm, and I wrenched it out of his limp grip, opening faint gashes in my arm.

"Who is she?" I snapped, glaring up at him.

His eyes flared brightly, and he exhaled from his nose, attention fixed on the thin two lines of blood on my arm. He made a move to grab me, but I stepped back. Was I jealous right now? I scoffed and shook my head, backing up . . . I felt possessive of him?

"You're the most feared in this area. Others avoid this sector because of you . . . and you're allowing a human to behave this way?"

I swung my stunned gaze to hers and scoffed.

"I'm not just a human," I snapped. *I'm his human.*

Thank God that didn't come out of my mouth.

The demoness's onyx eyes slitted, and her head dipped. All that kept replaying in my head were those sharp horns impaling my body. I cleared my throat and pursed my lips.

"I will tear you to pieces if you touch her."

She jerked back as if stunned.

What the hell was going on? She was so shocked by his behavior, as if she was used to more loving or gentler reactions from him. This was not good, and it caused this lump in my throat to expand.

"I'll leave." I wrapped my arms around my torso to contain my skyrocketing heartbeat.

Tene lunged forward, the movement so quick I yelped.

"No," he hissed, hoisting me into his arms.

His glowing eyes narrowed, and he shook me, unsteadying me. I flailed to grip his horn so I didn't topple to the ground, and he sucked in a breath. His body tensed, and I frowned as we stared at each other. I dragged my fingertips down the rough slope, and his breathing changed.

The demoness moved and he growled, sending her cringing back. He clutched me tight as he retreated into the cave.

His glow illuminated our room, and I stared up at him as his shoulders moved up and down in quick succession. I dragged my fingertips up his neck and past the sharp angles of his face, to grip into his horns. I flexed my fingers around the rough texture, and his shoulders shuddered. He stopped near the pile of blankets where we slept and fucked.

"Who is she?" I repeated.

He hissed, eyes flaring. "No concern to you. She will never touch you."

That was enough to him. No answer was needed.

I understood why. He was a monster. He didn't understand my emotions, but I wouldn't lie to myself. Frustration bubbled, and my fingers flexed around his horns, encircling it and rubbing downward to the base. Tene exhaled, the noise on the verge of being a whimper.

I repeated the motion.

"Who is she?" I trailed my fingertips along the arch of his horn. His mouth opened, and I had full view of his dangerous teeth.

His knees buckled, and he dropped onto the pile of blankets. His thighs cushioned my ass as he fell to the ground. Humming, I pulled my dress over my head, tossed it to the side, and kicked my shoes off.

The cool cave air puckered my nipples, and I hoisted myself up by his shoulders, resting my bent knees on his thighs. The height gave me leverage, allowing me to reach him so I could drag the flat of my tongue over a textured horn. He hissed. Could I make him come by touching them?

I wrapped my other hand around the other horn, caressing it. The four long tentacles unwound from his thick cock, and the softer insides grazed against my thighs. I flicked my tongue against the curved horn, and he sucked in a sudden breath, his ridged cock twitching against his belly—never becoming soft.

His hands grasped my waist, and his claws dug into my flesh, piercing me. I gasped and the harsh hold loosened. He'd punctured me, but it didn't make me want him less. I pressed my mouth to the side of his horn, swirling my tongue against the rough surface. Cum spurted from his cock, painting my stomach with its glow. The warm release slid down my stomach, dripping onto my mound and clit.

Tene's shoulders moved harshly with each breath.

"Who is she?"

"We spawned from the same demoness."

That . . . that meant they were siblings!

I was freaking out for no reason! Ugh. Heat flooded my cheeks, and he stared into my face.

The back of his hand lifted to my cheek.

"Are you well? Your temperature spiked."

I cleared my throat and nodded.

No way would I admit my embarrassment. His head tipped

to the side and his eyelids narrowed, blocking some of the glow. I licked my lips and looked down at my cum-painted stomach.

I rubbed the liquid on my fingers and lifted them to my mouth. My eyes slid closed as I sucked on the appendage—savoring the sweet, mouthwatering taste. I'd racked my brain and finally figured out a comparable taste. It was like the best, most flavorful blueberries. Refreshing.

I hummed and dragged my finger across my stomach until my fingers were covered in the glowing cum.

"Do you like my release, my human?"

Seduction bled from his tone. This was the most playful I'd heard him.

He gripped my hips and lifted me to lower me to the ground in front of him. His large hand wrapped around my head, caressing my cheek while he lowered his head and his tongue lapped up the blood dotting my arm from his claws.

"Do you?"

I swallowed hard and nodded, mouth watering and sex throbbing.

"Take more from me, then." He hissed and slipped his palm behind my neck, guiding me to his cock. I parted my lips, sucking the tip of his dick into my mouth.

Relaxing my jaw, I angled my head, managing to get two knots stuffed into my mouth. His tail trailed over my thigh and between my legs. My channel fluttered as it caressed my clit—nowhere near hard enough.

I whimpered and wiggled in place, but my movement stopped when his hold on me tightened.

My hands lifted to wrap around the rest of his cock, dragging down the slick wet shaft. Up. Down.

He snarled, head tipping back as his hips convulsed.

I stayed in place as he fucked my mouth, his hips moving in circular, incremental pumps.

SHE WAS INSATIABLE. NEEDY FOR MY *CUM*—AS SHE called it. So I fed it to her. I wanted to keep her by my side as long as I could because this human was different.

The glow from my cock illuminated her face as my tentacles wrapped around her jaw, caressing her.

Her sweet scent permeated the air, filling my senses, and a quiver worked through my limbs. The same one seeped from her when she wanted me.

Pressure accumulated at my spine and legs, increasing with each of her licks. I thrust my tail into her warm depths, swirling it in circular motions, which seemed to enflame her.

Her mouth on me shook my foundation, as if my body was injected with life every time she neared me. The organ that pumped me with life rested in the middle of my chest and continued to behave abnormally.

Was this . . . emotion?

"Come for me, baby." She breathed against the tip of my moist, turgid cock. I stilled for a beat, then erupted. Her mouth opened, catching the jutting release. The sleek line of her throat fluttered as she sucked down my essence, but it was too much for her to handle and leaked from the corners of her mouth, down her chin, and over her breasts, coating her nipples.

Good.

Bridget pulled back and cum jutted across her neck, painting her skin with glowing streaks. Covering her more than she already was. I liked it.

My . . . cock wanted her always. I needed her with me *always*. A purr trembled through my chest.

I forced her onto her back and rubbed my release into her skin, spreading it over her flesh until a thin layer glowed from her pussy up to her neck.

I zeroed in on my onyx claw raking across her flesh and the small bumps I left in my wake. Her eyelashes lowered, each blink slowing.

When her lips turned up like that . . .

That constricting in my chest elevated, electrifying my limbs.

"Do you fear me?" The query came without thought, but I could not figure out this human. She had feared me, but she did not behave as she did. She did not run from me.

A small dent formed between her eyebrows. Her hand slid up and wrapped around two of my fingers, and she smiled as her breathing became even and low.

"No," she panted. As I thought. I marveled at her. She did not fear me.

Her mouth stretched with that exhale again and her eyes fluttered, shutting. Mumbling words slipped from her mouth. "I like you." A hum I'd never heard came from her, and it caused a constriction around my chest.

Like?

What was that word? It caused a thickness in my throat. I should have studied humans more, or incorporated myself in monster societies somehow, they must know what this meant.

All I knew about humans was inspiring their fear . . . but she didn't fear me.

A heated throb pressurized my chest, and I quaked.

Watching her—I would never tire of it, which was why I needed to keep her by my side. My body ached when I was away from her.

A familial scent mingled with my human, and I gritted my teeth.

Elbri.

I lifted with stealth and crept out of the room she rested in. Elbri waited at the threshold, leaning against the wall. I bared my teeth and stilled. Elbri flirted with death by remaining after I'd ordered her to leave.

"Why are you treating her as a pet. Humans are best eaten alive and fighting for their life. If you wait any longer, you shall have a meaningless meal."

I focused on her careless lean.

"Meaningless. What do you mean?"

She lifted her claw near her face, observing it as she spoke.

"Humans do not survive long in our atmosphere."

Every muscle in my body spasmed and the odd thud in my chest quickened.

"So let us kill her, Tenebrous—"

"She is *mine* to kill," I hissed. The idea of another having their claws on my human was unacceptable.

Elbri sneered. "If you don't kill her, I will."

Rage burned through my runes, and then I was in her face with my claws gripping her as I pinned her against the wall.

"She is mine." Elbri did not move or speak. Desperation forced my next words free. "Is there any way for her to live?"

She clicked her teeth at me.

I took that as my answer and sank my claws into her throat. She struggled until I buried them deep.

"Leave here and do not return."

She shivered and lowered her gaze from mine. Extracting my talons from her throat, she dropped to the ground. Onyx blood dripped from my claw tips as she slunk away.

She would not return. Elbri was nothing if not a coward.

Her words played in my head. If she would not survive in my atmosphere, how long did she have left? My chest felt like something had smashed into it repeatedly. There had to be a way to keep her with me. I could not lose her.

I quieted. There was no change to her breathing. She continued slumbering.

Elbri would be long gone now, but another monster may have answers. There were often creatures bordering my territory.

Without a moment to lose, I rushed from my cave to search for any creature I could encounter. I did not care which type. I raced up the incline, exiting my cave, and toward the trees. Many had to travel past my territory, and this marked the border outside of my area. A squat wart creature waddled near a stream, and I crept close.

It froze, and fear seared my nostrils.

"Do not run."

Yet, it ran. My sight blurred, and the next moment, I sank my teeth deep into the monster's throat.

I growled and dropped it.

I must break this cycle. Finding someone to answer my questions became priority but everything ran from me.

There was a place in the eastern land where a community of monsters sold humans. They had to have a way to get the humans to survive. I'd travel that direction. My cave remained well hidden down the incline, and all monsters knew not to enter my territory. My human would be safe until I returned.

Phrases . . . words . . . sensations arose that I had never experienced. It had been so long since I had been near others. Even the female demoness.

Humans do not survive in this atmosphere for long, but mine had. There had to be a reason.

If finding answers failed, I would move us to the human side of the Rift before she was taken from me.

It may be the only way I could save my human.

MINE TO KILL.

I sucked in a breath, sitting up as the words rounded my mind. I would die? The blankets bunched under my fingers as I scrambled to sit up. I blinked groggily. I'd laid still after the conversation I heard, waiting until there was no sound.

My head spun, and I waited a beat, gathering my bearings. I had to feel around to find my shoes and dress, trying to be as quick as possible. Damn him for being the only source of light. Once clothed, I pressed my palms into the cave surface and felt my way down.

Where had he gone after talking about killing me? My throat clogged again and panic crept over me, making me freeze up, but I couldn't afford to waste time. I needed to run while he wasn't around . . . even though I ached to run to him and beg for him not to kill me.

The musty scent of rock I'd gotten used to filled my nose. It was worse whenever I went the wrong way, toward the pool in the cave. That told me I'd taken the wrong turn earlier. I backtracked and headed the correct way.

My toe banged into a pebble and sent it skittering. The sound echoed. The muscles in my neck tightened, and I rubbed them, trying to get rid of the uncomfortable sensation.

Think, Bridget.

Panic blinded me, but I knew better. I may have misheard or misunderstood. Sure, it was difficult to take that phrase out of context, but he *was* a monster.

"Tene?" I called out after a beat of hesitation. My voice bounced around.

I licked my lips, and inched down.

"You weakened him."

I screamed, flattening against the rock wall at my back. The eerie words were low and terrifying with how they held rage.

"He loathes you for softening him."

It was the female demoness. His sibling. She was still here— but where was Tene?

"What?" I said, hands on my hips, trying to stall for time.

Claws sliced into my arm and side, sending blinding pain through my body.

I screamed and clutched my wound. Blinking through blurred vision, I wheezed, shakily cringing into the wall.

I couldn't see anything, but I felt her presence nearing. My stomach dropped to the depths of hell when her breath caressed my cheek.

The punctures in my side and arm burned. I lifted my shaky hand to the wound on my arm, and blood wet my fingers, so I clasped it tightly, attempting to stanch the flow.

"You're a weakness he does not need." My adrenaline-riddled brain struggled to comprehend. "He is one of the most powerful creatures to exist, and you think you're enough?"

Tene . . .

"He wants to be rid of you," she hissed. My stomach roiled. Her words filtered through, finally stringing together in my brain.

I bit down on the inside of my cheek to detract from the hurt spreading in my throat.

"Y-you don't have to listen to him." I forced out through a trembling voice. Her laugh lifted the hair on the back of my neck.

No. Getting murdered in a painful way wasn't on my list. A renewed fire in my gut roared forward, and I drew my leg back in a quick motion, slamming my heel toward her voice.

In the same motion, I rolled, then sprinted with everything in me.

Her hiss reached my ears, but I focused on running.

Shit. Shit. I took the turn, following the path leading outside the cave.

The light guiding me outside glowed so close.

I had such a small opportunity of surviving, but it was nonexistent while in the dark. I cleared the exit, and a crack resonated behind me. It sounded like wood.

Fucking bitch! She smashed the bed base that had taken so much effort for me to build.

I dove for the serrated knife I'd left on the ground, and my momentum rolled me a few times.

Claws sliced into my arm, and I squeezed my eyes shut, slamming the knife upward. It sank into the soft section beneath her chin.

I screamed as blood spilled from her mouth. Her eyes widened, and she tried opening her mouth, but the knife kept it clamped.

My stomach heaved. I was going to throw up. Her claws slammed into my sides, and tears seeped from the corner of my eyes. She was going to kill me if I didn't do her in first.

But how would that happen if a knife through her mouth hadn't stopped her? I gripped the knife harder and pushed into the wound. It inched closer to her neck, causing a large wound from under her chin to her throat.

I grunted and continued shoving, using all my might to jerk it down.

The squishy sound sickened me, but I ground my teeth together. Blood leaked onto my dress and splattered against my face, but I couldn't stop.

Her arms spasmed before she stopped moving, her head falling to the side, lifeless.

I panted as I shoved her off me and whimpered at the extraction of her claws, then scrambled back, hugging myself.

Dead. She was dead.

I killed Tene's sibling. Oh fuck. My stomach roiled and I flipped over. With each heave, I spat out bile. It was pure luck that I was still alive.

I'd done the same to Liam's sister, and he'd tied me to a pole.

If he hadn't believed me, I had no chance getting a monster to believe I had done it from necessity. I shuddered, tears leaking from the corners of my eyes as I returned my attention to the dead demoness.

The knot in my stomach tightened.

Mine to kill. If those words weren't true before, or if they were out of context—not anymore.

He would get rid of me.

Bile coated my tongue, and I heaved again before getting a handle on my anxiety.

What was I doing falling for a demon?

A MIXTURE OF DIRT AND PEBBLES CRUNCHED BENEATH my shoes. My thighs burned with exertion, but I kept pushing forward. A little farther, then I would stop to rest once I found some coverage. Being out in the open put me on edge like no one's business.

Everything was so foreign, and I doubted I was safe anywhere, but at least I could get coverage from the foliage. I hoped to God I didn't run into anything. Swiping the sweat from my temple, I wondered how long I'd been walking. I couldn't even tell because there was no sense of time or direction.

Maybe I shouldn't have taken off like a bat out of hell, but there was no use in waiting around for him to kill me.

But what if he wouldn't have killed me?

Useless hope. Childish, and I knew better. Liam taught me how easy it was to turn your back on someone.

I killed Tene's sister. I'd seen the possessive way the demoness behaved. For fuck's sake, I didn't know their relationship. Was he even telling the truth? Or was everything a ruse to play with me? There was no way he'd spare me. Anyway, there was no certainty he had fuzzy feelings toward me other than my fanciful hope. I was just a curiosity to him.

But the sweet care . . . and the gentle way he touched—No. It didn't mean the same to him as it did me.

I huffed and rubbed my pained stomach.

Scabs flaked my wounds, which was fortunate, since I verged on bleeding out there for a moment. It was another indicator of how my body had changed. Each step forward dragged a little more than the last, and I stumbled as I dipped through the trees. I didn't know where I was headed, but walking was my only option.

With an exhale, I beelined toward a sparse collection of foliage near a cliff. That stone would serve as a good place to rest. I trudged over a larger stone, my lungs burning with each movement, and I dipped to avoid a collection of dark wood with stringy tendrils hanging. The thick cluster worsened, getting into my face and tugging at my hair. Spluttering, I swatted it away and hunched lower.

My heart burned a hole in my chest, and it wasn't just exhaustion making it hurt, it was the circumstances. I'd grown to like the demon and shouldn't have. How could I be this tangled?

I puffed out my cheeks. What had I done? Being involved with a monster was not supposed to hold the drama that being with a human held, but here I was, worse off.

Continuing my momentum through the prickly stuff, I hugged my arms to make myself smaller. The foliage turned into a sort of tunnel made up of the bramble.

Shit. Was this a nest? . . . I quickened my pace, the end in sight. I burst out on the other side and smacked at a web that caught on my cheek. Shuddering, I patted myself down and backed away from the thick, overgrown foliage. After a few steps, I reached the stone I had my eye on. That tree overhead looked much larger than it had from afar and the surface had a vine consistency.

I brushed away the dust and bits of branch stuck to my dress, so determined to get the leaf off my shoulder that I didn't see the boulder until my toe rammed into it. Screaming, I toppled to the ground, landing with an ungracious thump.

What was the use? I whimpered and rolled over, blinking up at the blurred fog with the sky peeking through the awning, stringy trees.

I'd been lucky so far, so the universe had to toss in a wrench. I shuddered and puffed my cheeks out, trying to hold back the watering of my eyes.

A reptilian clicking had me tensing and my lungs seizing. I had to crane my head farther back until I was staring at slitted eyes and the snout of a dragon.

"What has you in such a state, human?"

I screamed and bounced to my feet, whirling to face the dragon. His rumbling voice vibrated across my skin.

"Worry, not. I will not harm you," he said. I blinked at those sharp teeth lining his mouth and gulped. Although Tene also had sharp teeth, they were, uh, smaller and less in your face. His tail flicked behind him as he pushed onto his hind legs, exposing his lean lower half that tapered down. The scales over his body rippled with each of his movements—the red shade striking. How had I not seen him?

He now stood like the dragons that had hauled me about earlier, but he was taller, putting him at about thirteen feet tall. Wings spanned out at both his sides, fluttering.

"Human," he muttered. The movement of his wings rustled my hair around my ears. I scooted backward.

This was such a stupid life—planet—world! Why had the San Andreas fault ruptured? Couldn't it have held off a good century until I lived my ordinary life out? I whimpered. I was not cut out for living through the end-times.

Tears leaked from my eyes. The dragon's scales shifted.

"Ah, exhaustion is kicking in. Must be your organs beginning to fail . . ."

Hold up.

I scowled. "What does that mean? Why would they fail?"

The dragon shook his wings out.

"Humans can't survive long in this atmosphere unless you drink of a monster's essence." He huffed a plume of smoke from his snout.

I blinked. Essence . . . did he mean what I thought he meant?

He must have read my shock as confusion.

"Our release, yes."

I coughed.

I was right. Tenebrous had been sustaining me with his cum . . . did he know?

"I can provide for you if you come with me."

He grinned wide. He'd just offered me his *essence*.

I gawked.

"N-no thanks." His scales rippled as he made an angry sound. Even though he seemed on the verge of striking at any moment, this dragon appeared to understand humans better than Tenebrous.

His wings beat, and he hovered off the ground, kicking up a flurry of dirt. I sneezed and cupped my hands around my nose, eyes, and mouth. Talons buried into my shoulder, wrapping around it as his wings beat and he lifted me higher and higher.

"No, stop!"

My arm burned at the joint, and I screamed, legs kicking. Flailing only made the pain worse, so I went limp. No point in trying to escape.

The wind whirled in my ears as he lifted me. Oh God. It was too high off the ground, and all this on my already abused body was not helping. My stomach roiled as the ground and I separated more and more.

MY EYES WATERED AS HE FLEW AMONG THE THICK purplish fog.

"Stop moving, human," he roared, but unlike the times Tene said it, it caused my insides to shrivel. My body seemed to lock in place as he lowered from the sky, unveiling the city below. From above, it looked like any other normal human city complete with skyscrapers. No way that was what I thought it was? The rounded ears of a notable roller coaster in Los Angeles poked into the fog, the metal structure tipped to the side so the ears leaned to the left. Rust and mossy growth coated sections of the ride.

At the bird's-eye view, it allowed me an overview of the other buildings. I'd heard about the Rift sucking in cities bordering the fault line from people that joined my ex-village, but seeing it was something else. Not even the old geography books preserved by our village put justice to the sight.

A green rusted sign was propped beside a building, the edges frayed as if a flame blower had been taken to it. *North 5* glinted on the sign, and the rest blurred from extensive damage.

The dragon's wings beat as we neared the ground, and the sprawling city blazed with flame-lit lamps. The flare cut through the gray-hued world. I yelped as the side of a building smacked my thigh, and I wiggled in the dragon's grip, which sent a wave of agony through my limbs.

A clear sight through the window of the sky rise left me gaping. Were they playing poker?

I blinked, astonished, unable to process the flashes of life around me.

The dragon's claws unhooked from my skin, and I stumbled forward, my legs tangled within my skirt. Dropping like a log, I whimpered. A burn in my thighs prickled up and down my limbs.

A red brick building loomed with light from torches illuminating the face of the front. A minotaur stumbled through the door, escorted by two green orcs.

I gawked, but that was all I could do before the dragon's claws sank into my shoulder and he dragged me down the slim alleyway, squeezing his body between the crevices. The towering building cast a shadow and there were no lights for me to see as I stumbled over cracked asphalt and vines.

I only kept on my feet because he held onto me. An intimidatingly large metal door stretched across the side.

He slammed a meaty claw on the surface, and a loud bang vibrated across my skin. The door swung open, and an orc stood at the threshold with his arms crossed.

"I'm here to see the naga."

The orc looked from him to me, dropping his gaze down my body and back up. I gave into the urge to hug my front even though my dress covered me well. He grunted and moved into the building.

"Go," the dragon ordered, and I raced up the step. The door thudded shut, and a lamp at the end lit up the long hall. My shoes rasped over the carpet. What had this place been before the Rift?

The orc turned and put his palm out, stopping our progress. I laced my fingers together and swept my gaze around. There was another door to the left a little farther down the hall, but that was it. I didn't know what was through there, but I debated making a run for it. I peeked at the dragon. I wouldn't get far enough.

This dragon meant no good; death glinted in his slitted eyes.

Licking my lips, I shuffled from foot to foot.

The door the orc went through creaked, casting a yellow light from within. He was only gone for a moment before a voice floated to my ears.

"Enter."

The dragon's claws wrapped around the back of my neck, then he shoved me into the room. I sucked in a breath. A monster behind the desk stared at me, and I froze as my stomach dropped. I may have pissed myself if the dragon didn't whack my back and send me stumbling forward. My knees hit the ground with an explosive grunt.

She stared at me from a reptilian, snakelike face, the glow from her eyes as bright as Tene's. The features of her cheekbones narrowed in an odd mix of snake and humanoid. Breasts bulged at her chest covered with sleek scales.

She leaned back, her elbows pressed into the armrests of her seat, and the end of her tail flicked beneath the desk.

"I could use her." Her slimmed face turned to the side. Even though there were no pupils, I could *feel* her gaze.

In a swift move, she tossed a small bag at the dragon, and he caught it. He grunted and backed through the door, leaving me behind.

My heart elevated to a dangerous level, and I whirled, but the orc slammed the door behind the traitor. The thump echoed around me, sealing my fate.

Oh no.

"Human. Sit," the snake woman said from behind me.

I bit my bottom lip. It didn't seem like a suggestion.

The orc grunted, and I avoided his glare as I dropped into the too big chair.

"As you can see, I own you now." My tongue stuck to the top of my mouth. "What is your name?"

The knot in my throat grew.

"Calm yourself. It's not as bad as you may think." The corners of her lips stretched, and her sharp teeth flashed. I may throw up. "I understand you may be shocked speaking with me, so I will have one of my girls explain things to you." She looked over at the orc. "Take her to Issa."

The orc tipped his head and waved me ahead of him. He wasn't going to manhandle me?

He grunted, and I scampered ahead of him. Amazingly enough, he held the door open as I walked through and waved a finger toward the only other door in the hall.

There was nothing I could do. I couldn't overpower them, outrun them, nothing. Monsters surrounded me, and the only thing to do was go with it until I found a way to escape—unless I wanted to die.

As soon as the door swung open, a flare of grunting, talking, and hissing sounded. Torch lamps lined the furthest wall from my vantage, which created a softly lit ambiance.

Booths and tables scattered throughout the space, all facing a wide black platform where a human woman danced seductively. She dipped with a twist of her hips and transitioned to the ground in a crawl.

Monsters crowed, some even standing as they hooted, grunted, or whatever noises they made.

The orc was already a few feet away from me, and I scrambled after him. The circular pattern of the floor led to tile. Machines with multiple numbers and shapes lined the walls and the unlit sign above a bar read "Casino."

"Issa," the orc said in a booming voice. A human woman in a short skirt and a bralette turned around, balancing a serving tray. Her gaze trailed over me, and awareness flickered through them. She grinned and nodded at the orc. She slid the empty tray on the bar top and flounced over, her skirt flaring around her.

She hooked her arm through mine and tugged me after her. She was much stronger than I'd anticipated with how petite she was.

"W-wait," I huffed, but she pulled me along, rushing through the booths and guiding me toward the side of the stage. A couple crossed in front of us; a woman and a minotaur cuddled while fondling one another.

They disappeared behind a wall as Issa led me through a room with a variety of clothing hanging over a rack, and vanities in a row. This was the most clothing I had seen in my life. Her fingers squeezed my wrist, and I avoided smacking into a girl fluffing her hair.

"I put my robe in the storage so it didn't get mixed up with the dancer's stuff. They get pissy if you get in their way." Issa made a face. "Here we are."

She flounced into a decent-sized closet and plucked a robe off the hanger.

"How is all of this possible . . .? Why is all of this . . .?"

"Shocking seeing it all, I know, but most of the monsters won't hurt you now that you're claimed."

"Claimed?" A metaphorical fist wrapped around my throat. "I don't want to be claimed." The only one I wanted claiming me was Tene. Stupid, useless hope.

"You will not survive without being owned." She said it so succinctly, leaving me speechless. It was obvious . . . but, shit.

My heart sped up, and I pressed my palm to my chest.

"I can't breathe."

"Oh no," Issa murmured, and she scampered around me and forced me into a chair. "Put your head between your legs."

I didn't have too much going on in my head other than panic, so I listened to the order. I bowed forward, and my nose bumped into my knee. I focused on breathing.

My life had shifted so much in a short amount of time and hadn't stopped changing.

"It's really not that bad," she murmured. "Especially being here and owned by Nikita. She's fair and doesn't force you to do anything you don't want." I scoffed, rubbing my cheek against the skirt of my dress. I pressed my elbows to my thighs, looking up at her.

"Monsters . . . how are they like this? Aren't they supposed to be wild creatures?"

Issa's eyebrows lifted, and she shook her head slowly.

"This dimension is too big to fit all monsters into one category." She brushed her fingers through her hair. "You're from a human village on the other side of the Rift, aren't you?"

I nodded slowly. "That's where most of our girls started off." She tsked and shook her head. "I forget how closed off some human villages can be. There are many that live in the 'old way.' They kill everything and anything that crosses their paths. But here, within the limits of this city, there are agreements of any who cross into it. Nikita owns this place, and she's built up her power and allies to do as she pleases. A key way she's done it is by offering humans."

I rubbed my palms on my eyes.

"It's just all too much."

"When monsters lived in their dimension before the Rift, they weren't cognizant. They were primitive and instinctual. But after the Rift, they gained self-awareness. All of this was a gradual shift. There are some monsters that want to be more civilized, and there are some that prefer being wild."

Tenebrous was the latter. He enjoyed his cave and being around no one and nothing.

"Coexisting didn't happen on a whim. It was a gradual process. It first came with the realization that monsters enjoyed how humans taste."

"I thought *we* needed their, uh, essence to survive on this side."

"Yes." A smile tipped up the corners of her lips. "*And* monsters crave us." Her face pinkened.

Tene's reaction told me as much.

"Then what is this place?" I struggled to wrap my head around the new information.

"Monster pleasure services would be the best way to describe it." She tied the sash at her waist. "It's up to you to which level you'd like to work in. There are dancers, servers like me, feeders, milkers, companions—"

"Whoa. Companions?"

"Sometimes monsters get lonely." She shrugged.

Baffling. This was all so baffling, but at least now I understood why Tene seemed to enjoy eating me out.

"So I assume feeders, uh, feed the monsters."

"Yep." The red on her cheeks flooded down her neck. "It's not the worst. I did it once for a bit more currency. I wanted to get a nice outfit."

"What are milkers?"

"Slang we use for milking-humans. You know how we survive off cum?"

Holy fuck. I pressed my palms to my face.

"Humans have to ingest cum once every few rotations. Female monsters provide it as well, if you're curious—but obviously not as effectively as males."

Couldn't say I wasn't curious about all of this, but the throb at my temple was only worsening.

"I can't leave?"

Issa pursed her lips and frowned as she rubbed her neck.

"Right now, you are under Nikita's protection. She purchased you, right?" At my nod, she continued. "Without protection, you'll be snatched up and they can do whatever they want to you." She fiddled with the ends of her hair. "I'm telling you, it's not so bad here. Nikita isn't too hard on us. She just expects us to work for her protection. Your best bet with leaving is finding an owner, but many of us want to be here." She whispered the last bit. "It's not that bad here and you have more options than out there." She shrugged. "Anyway, let me take you to your bedroom upstairs."

I trailed after her, my brain too crowded to think logically. "I remember when I first arrived here. The first thing I wanted was to bathe and to change clothes. We have a private bathing pool for female humans."

She went the other direction where black stairs started instead of where we'd entered.

God, I missed Tene.

BRIDGET

Issa dragged me out of bed, much to my chagrin. Human women worked during certain blocks of time. I'd only been here one night and couldn't deny the relaxed vibe of all the women I encountered. Stifling my yawn, I stumbled down the eight flights of stairs.

"I want to give you the rundown of the city before your first shift tonight." I nodded, my eyes burning. I couldn't sleep last night at all. It didn't help that the girl I shared the room with snored, but at least I'd bathed and had a few new sets of clothing. "Also, if you encounter a creature that won't leave you alone, say you belong to someone. Don't pussy foot. Some crazy fucker can force a bond between you if he takes a liking to you." Bond? What in the hell was a bond?

The dragon at the door swept his gaze over Issa and me as we passed him. I swallowed the slew of questions I was about to launch into. Cool air brushed across my face as we stepped outside.

I rubbed my arms and nibbled on my lip as I looked side to side. A large shadowy cloud loomed in the distance. I don't know how or why, but I could feel the maliciousness from the cloudy puff. I swallowed hard.

"What is that?"

Issa grimaced and lowered her gaze to her feet.

The beating of wings rang in my eardrums, and a large bulky form slammed down beside Issa, and the ground vibrated with his landing.

"Our protection," she muttered, and her expression soured.

"Quickly," he grumbled. His skin was gray. Gray, gray, not bluish gray like Tenebrous.

And his flesh looked hard as granite, the planes of his face broad, edged, and rough.

Gargoyle.

"Do you hear me, Issa." How was the girl not trembling under his glare? It wasn't directed at me, and it shook me.

"Yes, yes, Vane, I hear you," she snapped and tipped her chin up, tugging me to walk after her.

At the edge of the brick buildings, the space opened to a cobbled street . . . and a sidewalk in both directions which led into the remnants of what I would assume was part of Los Angeles. I gasped, pivoting. The front of the building behind me was tall and "Library" was scrawled across the front. Two swinging doors adorned the front, and the open sign remained. My chin tipped up to the large clock at the top.

"A clock." I had not seen one other than in the scripts in our village. "W-why does everything look . . . ." Put together, how it was before—I didn't know how to phrase it. My chest throbbed seeing structures and materials similar to the world I'd lived in.

"Feels like our world, doesn't it?" Issa grinned at me, and I blinked to clear the moisture. It really did. Nostalgia smacked me across the face, and I cleared my throat, trying to get control of my emotions.

The low hum of chatting pulled my attention down the street where a group of humans and one monster strolled in the opposite direction. Was that one of those tree monsters? Holy shit, it was.

"Let me show you my favorite café." Issa tipped her head to the building on the other side of the street. There was no sign on this one and it seemed to be the same structural design as the library.

I followed her, clasping my side. My wounds burned more this morning than last night. That demoness had done a number on me.

The gargoyle remained near her, his gaze sweeping around. A long flowing material flitted around his body, fitting his large body perfectly. They had to have someone tailor them for their shapes and sizes. There were even slits for wings, and ties held the back together beneath the gray aggressive-looking wings.

The gargoyle stepped inside and held the door open for Issa. I quickened my stride, blinking the dots that sprouted in front of my eyes.

Inside was lit up by glowing lamps, even though the windows allowed the hue of outside to shine through.

Large monster-worthy tables spread in front of the counter where a red-eyed bug-looking creature filled cups.

I blinked but tried to keep my face expressionless. It was too strange for my brain to comprehend, so it was time to get my mind distracted. We scooted into a booth near the entry.

"When you said a bond can happen . . . what does that mean?"

"If they share their essence"—she cleared her throat—"for

an extended period of time with one human in multiple . . . ways, it ties their life forces together, which means the human's aging slows. That sounds great and all unless you're bonded to an evil one that hurts you. One of my friends escaped a situation like that." Issa wrinkled her nose as if recalling the details of her friend's experience. "But there are undeniable benefits—if you get a good one." I was definitely subjected to a few of those perks.

My face warmed and the heat spread down my neck. This was too much for my brain.

"What is the time frame?"

Was I now tied to Tenebrous? My heart thundered in my ears.

"Half a year is the consensus observed with other pairings." A stab of disappointment sliced into my chest because there was no way I'd been with him that long.

Other pairings . . . there were more human-monster couples?

"Have you encountered other pairs?"

"Yes . . . there have been a few," Issa said, clasping her hands in front of her.

And why did that excite me?

"Can the bond be broken?" My voice cracked, so I cleared my throat and forced my voice to lower. It wasn't like I had a monster. Not now that Tenebrous would want me dead.

"I don't know, why don't we ask Vane?" she said, smiling up at where he hovered behind her seat and lifted an eyebrow.

His nostrils flared.

"This is enough, time to return." We hadn't even ordered. I scowled up at him, but he didn't spare me a glance.

Issa's teeth clicked together, but she didn't put up a fight as she bounced off her seat.

"Killjoy can't see anyone having fun," she muttered. She tugged me back the way we came and released the café door in the gargoyle's face. I peeked from her to him. That sniping did not seem normal.

She stayed quiet, seeming to stew over something, on the way back. Vane directed us to the pathway I had first gone through, and the orc allowed us through the entrance again. We crossed Nikita's room, and a familiar voice stopped me in my tracks.

I gasped, bringing attention to myself.

No way.

Liam stood up so fast, his chair tipped over on its back. His eyebrows were high on his forehead and his breathing was elevated. Was he about to cry?

Liam jolted forward. His hands cupped my face and dragged down my arms. He was much shorter than I remembered . . . or maybe I got used to tipping my head back to look at Tene.

Another throb in my chest.

"I missed you, Bridget." I opened and closed my mouth. *What?*

I had no clue what he was getting at after leaving me to die.

I scoffed. His eyes overflowed with tears, and his fingers pressed into my arms, but I gripped his wrist and yanked myself from his hold.

"Someone came forward after you were gone and admitted Leila planned it. Bridget, I'm sorry. I'm sorry." His mop of hair fell into his eyes as he shook, lowering his head. "I was wrong."

"Live and learn," I stated.

"Everyone is gone, Bridget," Liam muttered. A tremble coursed over his shoulders. Man was about to lose it.

I slapped his face, and the sting radiated through my palm. "Snap out of it," I ordered. His comment left a lot to the imagination, but I was sure with him being here, nothing good happened to the village.

He sniffled, expression still crumpled. We had it easy in our little town. I hadn't realized how much of a wimp he was. It never clicked that he was never on any raids or that he never left the village.

"I missed you."

Oh God.

Nikita observed with her head tilted.

"How are you settling in? Have you decided what area you would like to work in?" she asked.

I shuffled foot to foot, looking her in her predatory, slitted eyes. "Yes, I would like to be a server like Issa."

"Wonderful." Nikita pressed her green fingers on the desk. "If you ever desire a change, let me know."

Issa grabbed my arm and tugged me away. Liam tried to follow, but the orc in the corner of the room grunted at him, and he shut his mouth, dropping in the seat.

I didn't pity him. Fuck him. I wasn't that good of a person that I could forgive him. Even all our years growing up together hadn't allowed him to spare me, so why should I?

TWENTY-TWO

BRIDGET

I stood back, staring at my uniform in the mirror. Even though I was stocked up on everything I could need—within limits—I couldn't rid myself of the dress hanging over the end of my bed.

I'd been skulking, but I had no chance to get over my wounds. There was no time to pause. Work started soon.

A light knock had me at the door within seconds.

"It fits perfectly," Issa said. I tugged the hem of the skirt down, and the thin biker shorts hardly grazed below my ass cheeks. I knew it was because every time we walked, the skirt fluttered and hinted at the skin there. "Didn't the wax leave you feeling good?"

My face warmed. She'd helped me wax everything. I'd never been so bare, and it felt different, but I kind of liked it.

"Yeah, I didn't realize what I'd been missing out on not going hairless."

She chuckled. I stepped out of the room and shut it behind me. The stairs were smack dab in the middle of the hall and led through the backstage.

"You don't look so good. You need to have some essence."

"No," I practically shouted. Issa lifted an eyebrow.

After finding out about the special properties in monster spunk . . . I understood I would need to drink some, but I wanted to wait until the last moment before I gave in. It was just, every time I thought about it, this throb overtook my chest.

Stupid of me since Tenebrous wanted me dead, but my body missed him. The pain in my heart? I didn't even want to think what that meant.

I licked my lips.

"I'll wait to have essence," I said in a calmer tone.

"If you're scared of creating a bond, that only happens when receiving it directly from the source." What was weird was thinking that every human here downed monster cum. "And *only* with each other."

"It's not that—" I cleared my throat. "I'm just not ready."

I hadn't talked to her about how long I'd been on this side, or about Tene, but she looked at me like she knew I hid something. I sucked on my lip as we descended and strode through the back. Multiple women were adorned with feathers, and they all looked at themselves in their mirrors. Issa leaned close so I could hear her over their chatter.

"Whenever you're ready I can take you to the nearest watering hole. They have my favorite dragon-flavored alcoholic drink, and they mix essence into it."

Dragon flavored? They came in different flavors?!

"Why can't we just drink it here."

Her nose wrinkled. "Here, we can only afford the basic swill that some low power monsters sell to Nikita."

I forced a smile.

"Let's do it."

"It's also a good place to scope singles out." I got the gist of what she meant in her smile. "There's this minotaur I've had my eye on." She shivered, eyes fluttering.

I laughed and followed her as she guided me through the floor and behind the counter. There weren't many patrons yet, but the show hadn't begun.

A shrill alarm rang. The vibrating, violent dings of a bell assaulted my ears. Patrons leaked out of one of the side doors.

Issa grabbed my shoulder and forced me down so the oversized bar blocked us.

"What's going on?"

"That means there's a violent uncontrollable nearby."

A crash ruptured through the lobby, and a shrill scream echoed off the walls. I was breathing so hard I couldn't hear myself think.

A familiar snarl sliced through me like a knife.

"Tenebrous," I whispered. Issa's eyes widened.

"Bridget, if you know him, you need to go hide! The guards will take the monster out."

My heartbeat skyrocketed.

I shot to my feet, gripping the edge of the counter for balance. His glowing runes blazed a few feet away, and my heart constricted. He was here to end me, but I couldn't help the rush of relief.

"If you shut the fuck up and tell me what you want, we can solve this," a gargoyle roared.

I stumbled around the bar, still holding onto it for balance.

"You have *my* human."

Tenebrous. Hearing those words again constricted my throat.

"I'll slaughter everyone here if you do not. Give. Her. To. Me." I couldn't let anyone get hurt because of me. Tenebrous was one of those monsters that resisted change, keeping to themselves, those that viewed humans as food or a product to own. He was kill first, don't ask later, so he didn't care about learning more or trying to assimilate into anything he was not used to. I couldn't blame him for his nature.

The gargoyle laughed, and my eyes widened. He underestimated Tenebrous's ability.

"Stop," I shouted, and shot off directly at him. His glowing eyes blazed and his runes flared brightly.

Looked like this was the end of the road for me.

IT WOULD BE OVER ANY MOMENT.

Claws grazed my arm and continued around me until I was flush to a wide, hard chest.

He . . . hugged me?

His nose dragged across my hair, and my eyes popped wide open.

"Human," he said, hissing low near my ear.

He trapped my arms at my sides, so I was just left gawking up at him. The knot in my throat throbbed as I took in the planes of his face. I couldn't read his expression, but the way he touched me was almost reverent.

The muscle in his jaw fluttered. My legs swung side to side as he clasped me to his chest and backed away from the approaching orc.

"You're not taking her. She belongs to Nikita." Vane stepped forward, and Tene whirled so fast my head spun.

Another orc joined, and then three more monsters appeared, all surrounding Tene. My fingers dug into his shoulders.

"Mine," Tene hissed, and the light leaked from his eyes, leaving them pitch black—scary. His claws sliced into my thighs, ripping my new shorts into ribbons. Tene forced my legs wide, onyx gaze not focused on me as he sneered at whoever stood in front of us. Suddenly, his glowing cock slammed through the shorts, tearing through them as he fed his bulbs into me.

"T-Tene," I screamed, and struggled to breathe as I dug my fingers into his shoulders.

Claws pricked my spine as he held me to his chest. His warm cock pulsed in my pussy, and his tentacles fastened around my thighs, gripping onto me for dear life. Heat flushed through my belly, and my clit pulsed.

A moan crawled free, and the walls of my channel flexed. A low threatening hiss exploded from his mouth.

He was prepared to have me attached at his cock as he fought them.

"I paid for her, creature," Nikita announced. I panted, pressing my cheek against his chest. She came slithering forward.

Tene's eyes narrowed, and he approached. I sucked in a breath, clenched my thighs at his waist, and waved my hand to block his sight. I'd seen the vicious look in his eyes before, and if he went on a killing spree, everyone would be in danger—including the humans.

"No," I yelled. "Do not hurt anyone, Tene." His jaw feathered, eyes flaring brightly as he focused over my shoulder. "Tene!"

He dropped his attention to me.

"You protect them?"

I scoffed, shaking my head. *That* stuck out to him?

"Don't hurt anyone. They helped me." That still didn't seem to sate the anger and he remained stiff, on the brink of attack. "They kept me safe."

Okay, that got in. His enraged face relaxed.

"I need to talk to him," I announced, hoping the snake woman would back off. I held my breath. She had no reason to listen, but by the narrowing of her eyes, she debated it.

"I will trust you to not escape, human. There is an unused floor on the left wing." Nikita snapped her fingers. "Show them to it, Issa."

Footsteps rushed forward, and I squeezed my eyes shut, wiggling in place. Heat seared my face from both embarrassment and arousal. Tene's cock twitched, and I sucked in a breath, peering up at his flared eyes.

"Let's go," I said, tipping my chin up. His glow returned and he grunted.

How did he seem so unbothered by his dick buried deep inside me?

Each sway of his hips jolted his cock in my channel, and I shuddered.

Tene cupped my ass and dragged me up, propping me tight against him. With pleasure slicing into me at every step, I could hardly feel the puncture of his claws.

I couldn't handle the suspense anymore. What would he do to me for killing the demoness? He didn't react as I expected—he never did. Was he drawing out my agony?

"I killed the demoness."

He froze as his runes flared. Only a moment of stillness went by before he hoisted me higher, a purr rumbling from his chest. I tipped my head back but had to shut my eyes since he was too bright to look at.

"Is this why you left me?"

I tensed, sucking in a lungful of air. My chest expanded painfully.

"Breathe, my human." His eyes flared, and he continued ascending with aggressive steps that fed his cock deeper into me. I kept my lips sealed as I battled with the increasing lust and fixed my gaze on his face. The sharp planes of his cheek seemed to be a steel line and it bunched as if he were clenching his dangerous teeth.

He hadn't killed me yet . . . A shadow cast over his face as he walked us into the hall.

I searched his features for anything to hint at his thoughts, but there was no use. Issa popped the door open to the twelfth floor. She flattened against the wall, but Tene didn't pay her any attention.

"The fifth door to the left is furnished," she called, and I didn't have the energy to look at her.

His runes illuminated the hall, guiding to where she directed us. It opened to a large square room. The walls were smooth, and in the middle was a simple bedframe with a mattress.

"Will you kill me for what I did to her?" I swallowed hard. I needed assurance. My voice bounced off the surfaces, echoing much louder than I'd meant.

The base of his nose scrunched.

"The fear coming from you burns my nose." His head dipped, and he sniffed near my throat. I tensed, sucking in a deep breath. Did he plan to kill me when I had my guard down? No, that didn't make sense because he hadn't held back with killing so far.

I blinked. His grip tightened before he lowered me to the edge of the bed with such caution . . .

Why was he so gentle?

His cock slipped out of me, and I felt his absence keenly.

Tene yanked my new shirt off my body and tossed it, exposing my belly. My hands lifted to cover my breasts. He inhaled sharply and dropped to his knees before me.

Four scabbed puncture wounds dotted my side, much shallower than the ones at my shoulder.

He hissed, light flaring from his eyes. Tenebrous brushed his fingertips over the wound.

"She did this to you?" I hesitantly nodded when he looked up at me. "If you had not ended her, I would have."

I exhaled, shuddering. Tears welled in my eyes, and I flexed my fingers at my arms. My shoulders lowered. He wasn't going to kill me or even punish me for killing his sibling . . .

The tension in my chest loosened a smidge, and I shuddered.

"How did you find me?" Tenebrous continued caressing my side. He dropped to his knees, peering at the marks on my skin. His long forked tongue flicked out to caress it. I let out a stuttered breath.

"I followed your blood until I lost track. After that, I searched everywhere nearby." He paused and inhaled so hard his chest shuddered. "I will never release you, human. You are mine."

"Oh," I panted. His claw continued to caress me, and now that I could relax, my body was thawing. I missed him so much.

Tene focused on my face and tilted his head. "What is this?" He sneered at the tears trickling from my eyes. Bringing his nose close, he sniffed my cheek. "Do not leak, human."

I sputtered out a hysterical laugh and his hands settling near my thighs caused the bed to dip. His forked tongue gingerly lashed across the moisture, stealing the tears from my face.

Tene enveloped me in his arms, and I curled my fingers on his chest. I grazed my nose on his pectoral, inhaling his scent. I missed his touch and his cock. His chest vibrated. "You want me," he crooned and cupped my chin.

I pursed my lips, nodded, and mustered up the courage to touch him back. His cheek fluttered under my fingertips, and I dragged my thumb across his lipless mouth.

I leaned forward and pressed my lips to him. His mouth was cool to the touch, and my skin was malleable against his leathery texture. Kissing him gently, I coaxed his mouth to move like mine.

He groaned, tongue sliding across my lip. It was thinner than mine, and dear God, the reach it had . . . I pressed harder against his mouth, taking care with his sharp teeth. His hands shook on my thighs, the pressure of his fingers tightening.

"I ache for you . . ."

He always touched me so reverently. My heart was about to explode.

"Fuck me, Tene." The words burst from me. God, I missed him so much. How was it possible to need him at this level already?

He stilled, then gripped my hips and plunged his cock into me.

A gush of wetness leaked from my sex, bathing his cock in my juices. He grunted, a sneer lifting his mouth.

Tene bowed over me to kiss me, his dick slipping out of my channel, so he could tongue my mouth with anxiety-ridden swipes.

His tentacles caressed my thighs, and I squealed, shying away from the ticklish sensation, but they firmly gripped onto the top of my thighs.

I lifted to my elbows for a better view of his blue glowing cock prodding my entrance. He slammed his hips forward.

I cried out from the fullness, and clenched my eyes shut, tears leaking from the corners. I missed this. I yearned for *him*, not just his cum. The last few days were tough fighting against that truth.

A slight glow shone through the skin at my belly where his cock protruded. He withdrew his cock to the tip and then slammed back into me. My head tipped back, eyelids fluttering. It hadn't been long since he'd fucked me, but it felt like ages. I would never tire of him . . .

He withdrew and slammed in again, grunting. He was so big that every slight indent of his cock prodded my clit with each movement. He lifted my hips, and I arched, crying out.

"I like that sound." He hissed and rammed into me again. My orgasm slammed forward, suspending my body until I couldn't feel my legs. My pussy fluttered around his cock, and I whimpered with each throb as I contracted around him. With my release came a rush of my moisture, and the tentacles dipped in and spread the wetness over my thighs.

He didn't stop fucking me.

One of the glowing tentacles pressed into the bud of my ass, forcing me to open more. My head thrashed side to side. So many sensations.

Another tentacle prodded into my pussy beside his cock, stuffing into me. Tene hissed. His eyes squeezed shut, blocking his glow as he grimaced, teeth flashing.

Seeing him so affected turned me on more. A tentacle

stuffed itself near my clit, so the pressure sent me into a violent release that had my ears ringing. He was perfect—and mine.

I ground my hips in a circular twist. More. More. More.

Tenebrous roared, head tipping back as his cock jerked inside me, squirting so much cum it dripped down to the bud of my ass where his tentacle burrowed.

My fingers were so tightly curled that they'd gone numb. His warm cum continued filling me as he panted, breaths ragged. He collapsed forward, catching himself on his palm as his heaving chest hovered over me, while his pale hair fluttered around his shoulders.

His face remained strained as he heaved until his breaths evened out. I would be happy just watching him.

"I made a mistake." I tensed up. He frowned, opening his eyes, the glow simmered so I could stare into it. "I do not want you to be confused and run from me again."

"What—"

"I left you alone to find a solution. Elbri informed me you would not survive in this atmosphere."

"Uh, about that—"

"I cannot lose you." He sneered and his grip stiffened.

"It's your cum."

He blinked slowly, head tipping to the side.

"Your cum helped me survive the atmosphere." He blinked again. "They even have a clinic in the city where monsters donate."

That jolted him. He became unnaturally still. Five seconds went by and then twenty. Time continued to pass until I couldn't keep track. Tenebrous's nostrils flared, and it was the trigger to get him out of whatever stupor he'd been in.

"Monsters donate cum . . . Did you?" A hiss slipped free at

the end of his sentence. His fingers dug into my shoulders as he slammed me higher on the mattress. He leaned over me, his hair waterfalling around my face.

"What?" I tensed and squinted through the flare of his runes.

"*Whose*," he spat, seething as he pressed his palm over my neck to force me to look at him. "I will slaughter them." His muscles flexed and eyes flared as he hissed, showing his sharp teeth.

A knot ballooned in my throat, and I couldn't breathe.

I shook my head, my hair flailing over my eyes.

"I didn't!"

He clicked his tongue, nose flaring.

"*My* human."

Tene licked my neck and dragged his tongue to my nipples in a caress. The domineering lick continued lower, until he hovered over my wet pussy. I'd never felt so claimed by a simple touch.

My chest rose and fell in a rapid pattern that increased as the forked tongue inched up my sopping slit.

Tenebrous lifted his head, chest moving in an enthralling rhythm. Staring at him left me without breath—I could do it all day. As odd and sharp as his features were, they still held beauty. His face lowered and he pressed his cheek against my damp core.

"The fur is gone," he murmured, his rough voice vibrating against my clit. I sucked in a breath as my hips twitched.

He dragged his head lower until he pressed his curved horn into me.

My thighs tensed and I attempted to rein in my hips, but I couldn't control them thrusting against the roughness of his horn. Tenebrous's shoulders shuddered.

He liked it too. Thank God, because I would not be able to stop myself.

I groaned at the texture and ground my pussy harder against the curved edge.

I tipped my head back as he continued rubbing his horn across my slit, and I whimpered, grinding against him.

Tene hissed, and the bed jostled. Was he fucking his cock into the mattress?

The bed shuddered again, and he moved his head in a circular motion, the roughness pressing against my clit. I cried out.

Yes, he was fucking it, and it turned me on.

TWENTY-FOUR

TENEBROUS

I ENJOYED WATCHING HER SLEEP . . . PROTECTING HER as she slumbered. She was exactly what I wanted, and I would ensure I was the same to her. Steps caused a creak through the hallway, and I shifted to all fours, creeping out in preparation to destroy whatever encroached on my Bridget.

Inhaling deeply, I paused as the human that had shown us up here shuffled near the end of the path.

My low hiss bounced off the walls, and she sucked in a breath, back slamming into the wall. She directed her attention to me. Her hair was compact ringlets closer to her ears.

"Bridget is my friend."

My eyelids narrowed.

She was mine!

I crept closer.

"Not like that." She put up her hands. "We are friends . . . allies."

Ah.

"Goddammit, freakiest creature I'd ever seen," she

muttered, and I assumed she had not meant for me to hear that based on how low it was. "Uh, Nikita wants to speak to you."

I sneered.

The human "friend" cleared her throat.

"That was the reaction she expected, so she's right out the door." With that final statement, she crept away and disappeared only for the naga to slink in her place. I lowered to all fours. Having her so near my human . . . I dug my claws into the wood floor.

"You've cost me money."

I hissed at the naga, and her head tilted. She was clothed— like humans. She was one of *those* monsters, choosing to be around humans instead of living in the old ways.

"We both know well we protect our own, demon, but you are outnumbered. If you attack, we will eventually manage to kill you and then your human."

A rattle vibrated in my throat.

How dare she.

My physique stiffened to a painful extent.

Never.

I hissed.

My human's death . . . I did not like that thought, and it caused an odd tightening in my chest.

A throb radiated outward from the appendage that pumped blood throughout my body. I pressed my palm to the ache, rubbing roughly.

"Have you bonded yourself to the human?" I did not like those analytical glances.

My shoulders jerked, and I narrowed my gaze on her.

Bonded to her?

The muscles in every limb tightened.

I didn't know what that meant, nor did I care, but what I did know was I never wanted my lotus to face anything that frightened her. I wanted to keep her safe and to touch her—always.

She was all that mattered.

"Take my advice. Humans enjoy comfort. They are pets that need a space to themselves." Comfort. "You live in the old ways, before the Rift, but there are other options. Civilized options—"

"Civilized." I scoffed. "You mean domesticated."

The naga's tail rattled at the end.

"If you will not listen to reason, you must trade with me to take her."

"Trade?" The statement was madness; what did she want from me?

"She owes me."

"She bought me and offered protection." My human's sweet voice fell to my ears, and I was wound around her within moments, crouching closer to the ground. "I owe her."

"The human has integrity."

"How long will it take to work it off?" Bridget focused on the snake, steel in her gaze.

"About ninety sleep cycles."

Bridget wet her lips and nodded.

My teeth clicked together, and she tugged my hair. I stilled in shock at the sharp stabs to my head from her pulling it.

"Stop, Tene." She stared at me with watery eyes. I curled my fingers to stop from clutching onto her.

"It's a plan, but can we stay on this floor?" There was a careful tone to her voice I had never heard before.

"I am not unreasonable. That is fair, human." The naga's

mouth stretched at the edges, and she slithered away with a final look at me.

My human backed up to the room and lay on the soft surface she'd slept on.

Bridget groaned, rubbing her cheek into her palm. I settled beside her, staring down at her as her eyelids fluttered open.

"Am I yours?" I murmured. Alarm flashed across her expression, and she straightened into a sitting position.

"I-I?"

She pressed her lips together, eyes flicking from side to side. Her face flushed, and her fingers flexed in her lap.

"You are worth more than my life." My nose flared. "I cannot bear separation from you. I want you in my space—always."

The redness on her cheeks spread over her nose, and my cock woke, lifting to press to my stomach so I could fuck her again. I pressed her to my chest.

As if with a mind of its own, my tail slipped up her bare leg and wrapped around her thigh. I yearned to be connected to her, so I slipped the tip of my tail into her tight pussy. The walls of her warmth fluttered around me, and my runes brightened up the space. A light floating sensation billowed in my chest and continued to expand. I craned my head down to look at her small human features.

The tipped chin and the parted lips . . . I couldn't think of a time where I wouldn't want to look at this human.

She belonged with me.

I STILL REELED FROM HIS WORDS, SO MUCH SO I couldn't fall asleep after his announcement, so I lay here, staring at him for who knew how long. Tenebrous's arms flexed around my waist. He'd curled himself around me like a snake, pressed as close as possible. His tail had wound itself around my thigh, the tip still burrowed inside me.

I peeked up at him from under my eyelashes. He made me feel so small and taken care of. I pressed my cheek into his hard, textured chest.

Everything he said—I felt the same way about him. Parting from him wasn't an option anymore. I wasn't sure when it happened or how I could have fallen, but I did.

I sighed, rubbing my nose into his leathery skin.

I was supposed to get to work to prepare the tables with Issa, so I should get a move on it, but first, I had to extricate myself from his hold.

His claw curled into my skin, and I wiggled so there was a small space for me to free my hand. I used that arm to pull his fingers away, one by one, until I could slide free.

His tail remained, so I pressed my lips together and reached for the tip stuffed inside me and tried to keep my body still. Despite my efforts, my channel fluttered, fighting to clutch onto him.

I squeezed my eyes shut and wrapped my hand around the tail to stop it from burrowing deeper. This wasn't the time to get turned on. His tail unwound from my thigh as I shimmied away, and with one foot on the ground, I quietly slipped off the mattress. His hands squeezed the bedding, and his claws clutched it like he'd been gripping me. His runes remained the dull low color they were when he slept.

Quickly moving, I tracked down spare clothing and shoes near the door. Issa must have dropped them off.

I gave him one more glance before escaping the room. Hopefully, he slept long. I rushed down the stairs.

A step creaked, and I paused, peering around, but after seeing nothing, I continued downstairs. The worst creepy crawly sensation skittered over my neck, but I kept on my path. Blue flashed in the corner of my eye, and I whirled.

"How long have you been following me?"

Tenebrous continued toward me, lessening the space between us until he invaded my space.

"You can't come with me. Just wait in the room, and I'll be back." I didn't want to be late. "Go back, please and I will explain later." I picked up my pace, the thud of my steps loud.

Even without hearing him, I was sure he still followed. I whirled midstep. He remained a foot away from me and stared down without expression.

"You have to stay," I said, exasperated.

"I will go where you go."

My chest tightened from the statement.

"That's not how it works, Tenebrous." I cleared my throat.

Tenebrous tilted his head.

"I don't understand."

I pressed my lips together. He was so damn precious. I shook my head. *Get it together.* If he came with me—I couldn't imagine how he would behave. What if he ate someone?

"You need to stay here, and I will go over there. When I finish working, I will come back. I won't disappear, Tene." I rubbed my palms against his warm arms, craning my head to look up at him with a forced smile.

His expression tightened, and his sharp teeth flashed with a grimace.

"I will see you later. Stay."

I stepped a few feet away and looked over my shoulder. Tenebrous remained in place. I sighed, *good.*

An orc stood sentry at the base of the stairs, and he watched me as I rushed past him. A moment later, a familiar hiss had me skidding to a stop.

Tenebrous held the orc from the throat.

"No!" I shouted and jumped, hooking my arms around his so I hung off him. "Tene, stop. Please." I needed something more to get his attention. I kicked, and my toe slammed against his leg. *Shit!* Was he made out of stone?

I whimpered and my grip loosened. Before I slammed onto my ass, he caught me. I hugged myself to his chest as the lean orc scowled from a few feet away. Tenebrous hissed, but I clapped my hands at his jaw and forced him to look into my eyes. It hurt with his eyes so bright with aggression. He must have realized because they dimmed.

"You can't do that," I snapped, exasperated. His eyes narrowed.

I pressed my palm to his chest, rubbing my thumb in a circle. I needed to put this differently because none of my arguments were clicking.

"You make me sad when you attack others," I muttered.

His shoulders jerked.

"Sad?"

He said the word, as if rolling it around in his mind. Not like he didn't know what it meant, more like he never felt it.

"I understand you need to feed, and I accept every part of you, but I need you not to hurt or attack anyone," I commanded. To my ears, my tone sounded similar to when a child was being scolded, but I leaned into it. His thin mouth curved down at the corners, and he backed away.

Guilt clenched my chest, but I held in my need to touch him. He snorted out a breath and backed up.

Before I gave in, I turned on my heel and rushed through the door, where I slammed into Issa. She grunted, and I caught her arm before she went flying back.

"Finally," she huffed out. "I was debating coming up to get you, but that demon of yours creeps the fuck out of me. Especially when he crawls around on his hands and feet."

I frowned, narrowing my eyes. Yeah, it was off-putting, but that was my demon. Issa lifted her hands. "Not that it doesn't make him hot."

Scoffing, I shook my head.

"So, what are we doing today?"

"Same deal, but we have another trainee." She grabbed my arm and yanked me toward the bar. We wove around the slowly moving trunk. "Don't stare," she hissed, and I averted my gawking. That creature had attacked me in the woods. Well, not exactly that one, but it was an arbol.

Liam slumped next to the bar. *Uh, no. Not him.* But it was useless to hope, considering the uniform of long black slacks and a mesh shirt. He perked up when he saw us coming. I lifted an eyebrow.

"Wait here for this next guest. He can be touchy. He knows he can't get away with it with me, but you're new meat." She whispered the last part.

She picked up the tray holding a large glass with golden-brown liquid. The feline male with stripes watched her approach his table with his pointed ears twitching.

His striped tail flicked near her ankle, but it hovered as he smiled with sharp teeth in his mouth.

"Bridge," Liam said and cleared his throat. I angled a glare at him.

"Don't speak to me," I snapped. Before I could say any more, the bartender placed two mugs on a tray.

"Where is Issa?"

"Not here," I said, and climbed the steps so the bar was at eye level. Considering the monster's height difference and the height of the bar, they had to place steps for us humans. I leaned my elbows against the wood.

"You take it, then, table three," Rory, the human bartender, said. Tattoos covered every visible surface of his skin, and he had a concentrated expression on his face. He also didn't talk down to Issa like the other bartender did.

Fortunately, I'd gotten the tables memorized yesterday, so I balanced the tray and stepped down without mishap.

Footsteps pounded after me, and I sighed, shaking my head.

"Bridget," he muttered. "Why won't you talk to me?"

The bags under his eyes were dark, and the whites were red-rimmed. I quickened my pace to table three.

The tabletop reached the middle of my breasts, and I carefully placed the mugs on the table.

"Need anything else?" I asked, smiling.

"No thanks," the female orc said, cuddling up to the male human. I smiled and backed away, holding my tray.

I kept my attention forward. If I didn't pay Liam attention, then he'd leave me alone.

"Stop following me," I muttered and stopped at the base of the bar stairs.

"I miss you. I miss us." He brushed his hair back. "Does our past not mean anything?"

"You tell me." I smirked.

"Yes!"

Well, the sarcasm flew over his head. I exhaled slowly. Seriously?

"You tied me up and left me to die, you creep."

"Bridget, need you up here," Rory called. Tenebrous's glowing form dragged my attention to him as he approached.

Shit.

"He will kill you if you keep it up," I hissed, and whirled toward Rory to place the tray back on the bar.

Don't act suspicious. *Don't act suspicious.*

I straightened my shoulders sand rounded as far away from Liam as I could.

Tene's glow flared from behind me, illuminating Rory's face.

"I'm going to need to leave," I croaked.

I wasn't sure if it was the expressionlessness or his constant hissing that made everyone pause. Pounding down the steps, I intercepted his narrow focus on Liam.

"Who is the human?" *Shit.*

I sighed and rubbed my eyes.

"No bloodshed, Bridget," Rory warned.

Shit!

I scurried after him as he neared Liam who gawked up at Tene.

"Who is this?"

"No one, Tene," I said, and wrapped my arm around his murdering-happy arm, inching myself in front of him.

"Lies."

"Okay, okay. He was just someone that I was close to."

I hooked my arms around his, unsuccessfully pinning them. Why was he this wide?! Either way, he'd have to brush me off to do anything, and time was better than nothing.

Tene hissed, his glow flaring. Liam stumbled backward.

"Don't, Tene. He doesn't matter anymore. I have and want you." Damn, he wasn't listening. "Remember our talk!"

That stopped him.

His mouth lifted in a sneer. "I will let you know now; I will not touch another. I am incapable."

My heart was about to explode.

"Good," I muttered, clearing my throat and trying to keep my cool while my insides wiggled like an ecstatic girl.

He tensed and directed his attention to me.

"You must never touch another." His claws flexed. "If you ever touch a male or female the way you touch me . . ."

Shit, he was going to lose control.

"I don't want anyone else. You're mine."

Tene's head tilted.

"I . . . am yours." The words were hesitant, but I nodded even though it wasn't a question. His tail wrapped around my ankle, and the corner of his mouth tipped up in a semblance of a smile, but it looked more like a feral baring of teeth.

"Let's go," I muttered, lips pressed into his chest.

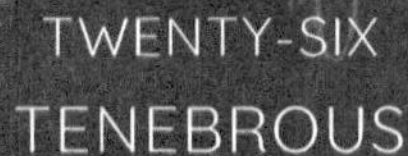

TWENTY-SIX

TENEBROUS

"I MUST SEE THE NAGA," I SAID THROUGH GRITTED teeth. The orc standing sentry at the base of the stairs snorted in a bhore-like manner, but I waited until he gave me what I requested. Seeing the leader of this place was the only way I could get Bridget away from here.

I refused to make her sad, which meant I could not destroy everything in my path as I craved. The orc exited through the entrance. This strange world was not something I was used to, but my lotus seemed to enjoy it.

The orc led me to a narrow pathway where another orc waited. They both walked me down to a rectangular box. I couldn't understand this need for symmetry. How was it so important to humans and domesticated creatures?

My blue light flared across my surroundings. Furnishings littered the area of every place I had looked, even in the soft material I fucked her on. Seeing her so comfortable—I wanted to give her that.

"What do you require to tell her she no longer needs to pay

off her debt to you?" The naga threaded her fingers together and leaned back. Her eyes flashed.

"Interesting, you demons are prideful, solitary creatures. I never expected for a human to wrap you around her finger." She bared her teeth.

"I lose patience," was all I had to say, and she rattled at me. She could be as angry as she wanted, but my goal was to get my questions answered.

Her head lowered and she stilled, contemplating. Her gaze roved down my form.

A silver trinket rested on the surface behind her, and the blue of my runes reflected off it. Treasures filled my cave, could she want them in exchange?

"Give me your essence," she said before I could offer.

I narrowed my eyes. Strange thing to request, but for my human, I would give anything.

"Fine. And I will take from you any comfort things I need for my human. We will continue to stay in the cave you have provided until I find a suitable location for her."

She smiled.

"Deal."

BRIDGET

As soon as my shift was over, Issa found me to tell me I no longer owed Nikita anything. I careened around to face her, and my hand fell off the bar top.

"Why?" I asked dumbfounded.

"She didn't say."

My eyes widened, and I dashed off.

"Bridget," Issa called after me, but her voice faded into the background of the chattering. Tene must have done something. *Please be in the room.* I huffed up the stairs, but he wasn't there.

"Tene?" I screamed, rushing back down. There was only one person he could have gotten to free me, and that was Nikita. The inconspicuous door to Nikita's office was unguarded, so I rushed inside.

The doorknob smacked into the wall, and Tene whirled. I raked my gaze over him, but he was in one piece. I exhaled and hurried to his side.

He was okay. I caught my breath as I turned to Nikita. She rested behind the desk with a large glass bottle in her grip. The glowing liquid was familiar.

"You are free to go." Nikita hadn't looked up at me, she popped the top of the bottle, and her eyes practically glinted. She dipped the tip of her pinky through the hole and lifted it. The glowing luminescent liquid glittered on her skin.

My breath was snatched from my body. She slowly brought her finger to her mouth, and it was an inch away from her tongue when I lost it.

Launching myself over the desk, I screamed and grabbed her finger and wiped the liquid away. She hissed and caught my arm in a harsh grip, but before she squeezed, Tene snapped the arm and clutched me to his chest.

As he dragged me close, I hugged the bottle.

"That is mine!" Nikita cried.

I sneered at her and tipped the bottle into my mouth, chugging it. I could only get a third down before I had to breathe. Nikita clutched her arm to her chest, her nostrils flared, and anger blazed in her glowing eyes.

"How did you get this?" I spat at her, so pissed that I didn't care I spoke to a monster like I could actually fight her off.

"He gave it to me."

I froze and looked up at Tene, betrayal glaring in my eyes. His mouth was slightly parted.

"How could you?"

"I bargained it for your freedom. It is worth much—"

"How would you feel if I offered my . . . *body* to someone else?" I snapped. "If they tasted me?"

His body jolted, and his arms squeezed me tight to him. A threatening hiss left his mouth.

"Mine."

His runes flared and dimmed, as they did when he experienced a strong emotion. An orc rushed into the room, and Tene backed away with a snarl as he clung to me. Blue leaked out of his eyes, and tentacles tangled with my thighs and then ripped my shorts off, leaving me bare. They tightened their hold, and Tene hugged me to his chest.

The bottle slipped from my grip and toppled to the ground, shattering. Tene grabbed my hips and lifted me before slamming me down on his cock. I gasped with each rutting thrust.

He stilled and hissed at something over his shoulder.

"Leave," he roared. A crash sounded, but I was too busy wiggling my hips to feed more of his dick inside me. The compression of one of his knots rubbed against my clit.

A pressure at the bud of my ass intensified. It was wider than his tail . . . a tentacle. It speared into me and wrenched a cry from my throat.

He pinned me to the wall, and his palms flattened my shoulders against it. A tickle at my nipple dragged my attention to his tail caressing me while his long tongue lapped the other one.

My eyelids fluttered.

An orgasm smacked into me, and my ears buzzed as everything faded, but he didn't stop fucking me.

I whimpered and cried and thrashed, but he didn't stop until I'd come so much my body was limp. Time blended and I didn't give a fuck where I was or who I was. His nose rubbed against my forehead, and a rumbling purr vibrated against my cheek.

"I did not understand what I had offered. I will not commit the same mistake again."

"You better not," I mumbled. He stepped away from the wall, and my legs wobbled as he set me on my feet. I worried my lip, and the nagging question burst free. "Did she touch you? Or did you touch yourself in front of her?"

He reeled back. "No one is to touch or watch me except you."

My shoulders dropped, and I brushed my hair behind my ears while heat warmed my face.

His tail lifted to caress across the bridge of my nose.

"I enjoy when you change color."

I snorted and cuddled close to him. *Oh shit.* There was a dent in the wall in the shape of my body. I grinned up at him.

"Get me out of here."

He got me out of there after we'd scrounged for some clothing in Nikita's office. No one stopped us, and every monster gave him a wide berth. It'd been because of me that he'd stayed, he always had the strength to get us out, but I'd stubbornly tried to keep my word.

Not anymore.

The travel time back to his cave was shorter than when I'd trudged across on my own. But it was likely easier because he carried me for all of it.

"We will arrive soon."

I peeked up at Tene. He'd become stiff, and his runes continued dimming. Something obviously bothered him.

"What's wrong?" I asked again, hoping he would answer. He looked down at me and then back up. His lipless mouth parted with a sigh.

"My cave does not have the human comforts you enjoyed."

That was what bothered him? I sank my teeth into my lower lip to hide my smile. My sweet demon.

"I have a solution."

I focused on him, but he didn't elaborate.

The terrain dipped on a familiar incline leading to the entrance to his cave. Elbri's blood still marked the ground, but her body was nowhere to be found. I didn't bother asking him about it.

He stepped into the cave, and the wet scent filled my senses. I kind of missed the deadly place. The jagged walls quickly passed with his stride until he entered a chamber. His glow reflected off gold coins within the cave. Piles and piles of it. I'd seen it in passing, but holy shit, I hadn't expected *this*.

I blinked, taking it all in as he set me down.

"We can trade this for your comforts." Jewels glinted various colors and intermingled with the gold. "Will this be sufficient, my lotus?"

"Y-yeah." I cleared my throat. I dropped my gaze to a smear on his side. I gripped his arm and peered closer. "You're bleeding." The split wound leaked onyx. It looked painful.

"W-what happened?" I mumbled. *Freaking out was counterproductive.* I repeated the phrase to myself but my pulse didn't slow. "Tene?" He didn't say anything, and I couldn't determine if he even heard my question from the lack of reaction. Fine, he could keep his silence, but I needed to get him cleaned up.

Licking my lips, I grabbed his arm, but he didn't even budge no matter how much I heaved.

"I need your help here," I snapped. My tone seemed to jolt through him, and he followed. Honestly, I wasn't doing more than wrapping myself around his arm as I guided him, but with him being a massive monster and all, I couldn't do much.

Last time I'd seen that gold, it had been near the waterfall, so it couldn't be far.

I scowled at him from the corner of my eye, irritated at his dragging pace.

The steady trickle of water echoed close by, and I stopped at the threshold. He yanked me to his chest, and my palm hit his lesion.

"I'm sorry!" I anxiously hovered my hand over his injury.

Ignoring me, he fastened his arm around my waist and stepped off the ledge. My stomach dipped, and I clutched him, squeezing tight. As soon as my feet settled on the sand, I dropped my arms. Thank God, I hadn't touched the jagged wound. I kicked off my shoes, shucked my clothes off, and gripped his fingers to guide him to the water.

"When did you get hurt?" Had he carried me the entire way while he bled out? This had to have happened during the scuffle in Nikita's office.

Tene said nothing. I glared at him and stopped when water caressed my waist. I cupped my hands to collect liquid and spilled it over his torso where blood painted his gray skin.

I needed to bandage it with something. My shirt would work if I tore it into ribbons.

"I'll be back."

Before I could move away, he yanked on my shoulder, and I tipped into the water. It splashed over my face, sending me into a spluttering fit. Swiping my palm across my mouth, I sucked in a lungful of oxygen.

"Don't leave." He scooped me up and hugged me to his chest, maneuvering me out of the water. "I need to have your taste," he murmured, and lay me on the sand.

His head dipped near my belly, and I gripped his horns. The tip of his tongue flicked out and brushed against my clit, and I twitched, my hips jerking up. Moisture rushed to my pussy.

Tene's mouth on me was heaven—he never failed to make me feel like he couldn't resist me. The power in that was enthralling.

Tene opened his mouth and the sharp tip of his teeth pressed over the mound of my clit, and he shoved his tongue into my pussy. He suddenly stiffened and his body trembled.

His removed his tongue and crawled up to gaze into my eyes.

"Are you well?" The words ran together.

I blinked up at him, panting as I forced a nod.

"You're bleeding." Horror tinged his words, and he gripped my face with both palms as he searched my face.

No fucking way.

My face warmed. I squeezed my legs together.

"Am I bleeding there?"

"Your pussy."

I cleared my throat.

"It's my period."

"What is this?" he hissed. "I will kill this *period*."

"No, Tene. It's my body. Humans bleed when they are not . . ." I searched for a word. "Breeding? Pregnant?"

He stilled and his nostrils flared.

"It is not hurting you?"

"N-no." Unless we were talking about cramps.

He relaxed and lowered down my body.

"Wait—"

I cut off with a squeak as he returned his tongue into my channel. My walls gripped onto it with throbbing pulses. He feasted on my core, unaffected by the blood. My legs went numb, and tingles shot through my spine. The orgasm surged across me with such suddenness that I screamed, arching my back.

Even the pressure of his talons at my spine stretched the pleasure.

"Mmm." A purr-like sound hummed from his throat as he slid his long tongue into my needy heat.

"How about three gold coins?" I met the gaze of the green creature huffing and puffing in front of his stand of cotton-filled bags perfect for stuffing a mattress.

"Listen, human, you cannot come here expecting your way —" My demon appeared next to him and wrapped his large claws around his face. An odd squalling escaped the goblin's mouth as he flailed a few feet off the ground. Tene's claw flexed around his head, and I hurried to grab Tene around the arm.

"No, Tene."

Black blood leaked from the puncture on the goblin's face. The noises from the market swelled, and a dragon stared over at us, very much judging.

"Not here, Tene," I whispered, and swept my gaze around. I didn't want to be run out of another damn market.

Okay, to be honest, Tene destroyed the last one, which meant we weren't *really* run out, more like, it no longer existed because my monster got too aggressive. Fortunately, that time, I'd purchased a few torches and fur blankets before everything went to shit.

I wanted a place to shop, and if he continued the pattern, there would be no options left. I wacked Tene's side, and his runes flared. I met his blazing eyes, and he unhooked one claw at a time from the goblin's skin until he dropped to the ground with a plume of dirt.

"Take it. Just take it," the goblin squeaked.

Sorry, I mouthed, and dropped the full number of coins he'd mentioned before I tried bargaining.

I shouldn't have done it; it wasn't like we didn't have tons of money. The stash Tene showed me was crazy and only the surface of what he had hidden in his cave, so gold wasn't a big concern—except the goblin tried to stiff me. I'd heard the price he'd given the orc before me.

I grabbed my bag of cotton and pulled Tene away from the stand before he killed—again. It was something I accepted about him. He was a monster and devoured whatever got in his way. Honestly, his primal reactions turned me on, but he needed to work on a smidge of self-control.

I rounded on him and shoved the burlap at his chest. His claws snagged on the brown material, and he stared down at it with the corner of his mouth tipped down.

"No killing," I ordered, and pointed my finger at him. He stared down at me with those glowing eyes. I turned on my heel, intent on getting out of here because it was looking like whatever semblance of restraint he'd mustered had run out.

Tene's claws tangled in my hair, and I stilled.

"Where are you going." The words sounded almost pouty in his odd hissing tone.

I yanked free and glared up at him. His tail tickled my calf and slid up to wrap around my thigh. A quick jerk had my breasts smashing the cotton between us.

His long, forked tongue glided against my cheek. "Do not be angry." His words vibrated through his chest. "I will please you."

That tail slithered its way higher, and I clenched my thighs to stop the progression. He'd fucked me in front of humans and monsters already, so I didn't doubt where this was headed if he continued.

"Tene," I chastised, and his head tilted.

"Do not be angry." His tail wiggled its way between the tight fit of my thighs, and the rounded tip pressed into my clit. I sucked in a breath.

He bared his teeth, but I recognized it was his version of smiling. My body softened.

Mischievous Tene softened me like butter over a fire.

There was no doubt he was a monster, but I'd fallen for his features. The rough skin, the horns, the pale long hair, and those glowing runes. Not even considering how much I loved his cock. That glowing appendage weakened me.

Tene's muscled arm wrapped around my waist as he released the bag, and he forced me so close my breasts smashed to his chest. My palm settled on his leathery skin.

He always considered my emotions even though he didn't understand them, and it made my heart squeeze with painful intensity.

"I love you," I blurted. Tenebrous flared bright and a clicking purr vibrated his chest. He couldn't understand the gravity of my statement, but he got the emotion behind it. Being from different worlds didn't diminish our fundamental understanding of each other.

He dipped to wrap his arms around my waist, hoisting me up so we were at eye level. His tail twined around my ankle.

"You are my everything."

A knot formed in my throat, and I pressed my mouth to his, taking care to not slice myself open on his teeth. His tongue slipped between my lips and skimmed against mine.

I never wanted to be apart from this monster.

ACKNOWLEDGMENTS

My alpha and beta team really pulled through and gave me the strength to finish DEMON when I needed it.
Rachel James, Kyrie Mangus, and Casey Roberts—you guys are the best.

Gina Cortez, you are an irreplaceable friend and critique partner. Thanks for talking me off the ledge over and over.

Another group of people I need to thank is my ARC team. You guys are amazing.

Gracias Ama y Apa.

ABOUT THE AUTHOR

Allie obsessively reads books featuring sexy, possessive heroes and headstrong heroines. So, it's no wonder characters just like that bustle to escape her imagination.

When she's not working away at her keyboard, she can be found in bed with a good book or bingeing shows.

* 9 7 8 1 9 6 5 3 0 0 1 5 2 *